What the Ocean Reveals

THE SECRETS OF BANYAN TREE BAY

BOOK 1

GRACIE GUY

Book Cover by Kris Norris

Editing and Formatting by Wendee Mullikin, Purple Pen Wordsmithing

First Edition, print and ebook: May 2024

eBook ISBN: 978-1-956587-19-7

Print ISBN: 978-1-956587-18-0

To GMR Sr. – always!

To Jennie – you've made so many steps in this life easier to bear.

Chapter One

Rivulets of sweat rolled down the side of her face while she sat still. The breeze was so faint only the highest peaks of the palm trees moved. A sauna—known as the month of July—wrapped her upper body. The humidity was like a heavy, wet blanket that caused her to take quick, shallow breaths. She wiped the glistening moisture from her upper lip. The fine, downy hair sprang up instantly, tickling her skin in the process. Then, she ran the paper towel across her cheeks and neck—but more sweat beads quickly took their place.

The plaintive call of the vocal blue jay was far in the distance. Much closer, she heard the scratchy voice of the mockingbird fill the late afternoon heat. To Willa, even the birds sounded hot. And she was sure her internal organs were in the process of being hard boiled.

Finally, a strong breeze swept across her face and arms; Willa closed her eyes and enjoyed the immediate cool-down it brought to her sweltering body. When she opened them, a bank of black clouds had snuffed out the blazing sunshine. She couldn't help but smile when the thunder started on one side of the building, rolling over it. The windows rattled in their metal frames; she held her breath, waiting for them to crack.

Moments later, big, fat, warm, ploppy drops of rain fell on her overheated skin. Standing up, Willa peeled off her tank top and lifted her face heavenward, enjoying the sensual beauty of the warm summer rain as it raced over her exposed skin.

"I'VE SEEN THAT LOOK BEFORE."

Tim turned to face the familiar voice. "Hey, Damian. How did you find me?"

"I put my brain into Northerner mode. Where's the first place most people from New York or New England come to when they get to Florida? The beach." His arm swung in a big arcing wave; fingers pointed across the vast expanse of water to where the setting sun would soon fill the horizon.

He stared at the near smirk on the face of his college roommate, Damian Buck.

Age hadn't tempered his quick wit or snarkiness. Damian was a man who lived on the edge—always counting on his tousled blonde hair and "good boy" looks to carry him through.

"Have you patented that line of thought, yet?"

"Ha, no. But I really should. Especially in the last few years. We've had so many Yankees move this way that it's a bit overwhelming. Everywhere I turn I hear accents from New York, especially Long Island, Boston, and Vermont. Ya'll are sort of pushing the Southern out of the south." He offered his hand to Tim, pulling him into a semi-hug, while clapping his other hand on Tim's left shoulder—classic bro greeting. "Seriously, welcome to Southwest Florida."

"It's nice to be here." Tim stepped backward out of the embrace, propping his hands on his hips.

"We've got lots to talk about. I think it's been at least ten years since we last saw each other. Where are you staying?"

Tim pointed to a small pink motel just visible past the fifteen-story national chain monstrosity staring down at them. "That little indie place."

"Ya know, I could have gotten you a deal here, right?" Damian nodded toward the beach-side tower. "A good friend—you know, the kind with benefits—is part of management there." His golden curls bobbed when he laughed.

Tim plastered on a slight smile and dipped his chin in one curt nod. *Do we even have anything in common anymore? If Damian has so little respect for women, it's definitely a sign we've drifted apart.*

"Yeah, it's okay. The little place is clean, the towels are soft, and the bed firm. That's about all I need to get me through until I find an apartment."

Damian pulled his phone from a back pocket and tipped his head up the beach where a heavy black cloud filled the sky. "Hey, that bad boy will be here shortly. Plus, it's pushing six o'clock. We're late for beer-thirty. There's a place about a block down from your motel that makes great grouper bites and hush puppies. And lots of cold beverages on tap. Shall we head out?"

"Sure. I might just as well get used to local food." Tim slid his hands into the front pockets of his lightweight shorts as Damian's arm went around his shoulder as they crossed over the hot sand of the main beach.

"Man, it is so good to have you here. And I can't believe you're not heading back north. Cool." His arm slid off Tim's shoulder when they reached the sidewalk.

Minutes later, a robust *whoosh* of chilled air greeted them as Damian yanked open the heavy wooden door of the Squawking Parrot.

Tim blinked repeatedly in reaction to the dark entrance hall, feeling as if he'd stumbled into a deep and musty closet. *Some ambiance.* But within a few feet, they stepped into a much larger and brighter room dominated by a center bar where three shapely young women were in constant motion, slinging drinks, passing food orders across the bar to customers, and even a little bit of side-hustle of Coyote Ugly-style dancing.

Damian led the way to a few empty seats on the far

side, dropping onto a stool, his back to the bank of windows facing the ocean. “Hey, beautiful.” He leaned forward to kiss a tantalizing redhead with long, wavy, to-die-for hair that curled under a well-rounded bottom covered in green boy shorts.

“Tim. This is Ariel.”

Snuffing out a soft chuckle, Tim suppressed the urge to ask if her name was real when she turned to him.

The comely bartender tilted her head, intense blue eyes locked on his before coquettishly glancing down, leading his gaze directly to the top of a pair of generous, alabaster breasts in a purple bikini top. The soft flesh bounced slightly when she giggled, prompting him to look up at her face. That’s when he noticed her extended hand. “It’s nice to meet you, Tim.”

“Thanks. The feeling is mutual.” Though his words were courteous, he let go of her soft hand as quickly as possible.

He struggled to keep his eyes from wandering. In the two years since his wife had passed away, Ariel was the closest thing to a naked woman’s body that he’d seen. *Wow, I didn’t know those parts still worked.* And, at that moment, the baggy shorts he wore were a blessing.

“So, what will it be?” Ariel directed the question to both men.

“I’ll have a shot of Gunpowder.” Damian pointed toward a top-shelf bottle of rum. “Make it a double, will ya Ariel?”

"How about you, handsome?" She leaned on the bar, her fingers lightly tapping on Tim's forearm.

"I'll take a pint of your best local IPA." He leaned back on his stool, intentionally breaking the physical connection. Before his marriage, his natural inclination had been to throw back a few shots, chat up the beauty, and make some noise. But despite what his man parts thought, Tim's head wasn't in agreement with them. Some of that had to do with missing his late wife, Nikki, but also, he felt he needed to maintain a level of control. It wouldn't be good for pictures of the new chief of police partying down to splash all over social media before he even started the job.

"Before you ask, yes, it's my real name."

Tim felt the flush of embarrassment fill his cheeks. "Your mom's a fan of Hans Christian Anderson?"

"You noticed!" Ariel spun around, smirking over her shoulder at him, she added a pronounced wiggle to her walk while moving to the end of the bar to get Damian's requested rum.

"Can I get fries with that shake?" Damian laughed loudly at his use of a thirty-year-old saying that should have died many a year before.

Tim shook his head at Damian.

"Hey Yankee, get over it. You live in paradise now. Why do you think they wear so little clothing? They love this shit. Believe me, I should know."

When their drinks arrived a few minutes later, Damian hoisted a fluted double shot glass of a deep red alcohol and tipped it toward Tim's glass. "Sláinte, my friend. Welcome to Banyan Tree Bay."

THE FIRST ROUNDS of thunder started just as Willa arrived home. As a local, the blow in–blow out nature of Florida weather was commonplace. And they had already experienced a few doozies. She hoped it wasn't a forecast for the fall frenzy of what she considered the real hurricane season. There were few things she dreaded more than hurricanes.

Putting her phone, keys, and bag on the kitchen counter, she crossed her flat to the bedroom to change her clothes when she heard her phone ping. *I swear, I cannot go anywhere without someone bothering me.* Sprinting back to grab her phone, Willa pressed her right thumb to the base to unlock the screen, hoping she wouldn't find anything urgent.

But the corners of her mouth curled upward at the blinking icon she found.

Hey babe. Hanging at the Parrot. Come meet my friend Tim.

After storm passes.

Come on. Scaredy cat.

Nope. Smarter than you.

K C U then.

Laughing, she took her phone with her to the bedroom. He was always Mr. Fun Guy. The class clown, with his "never met a stranger" ability to converse. And never once did he fail to draw people in—regardless of the topic.

Willa's thoughts about Damian floated through her mind as she peeled off her bra and panties.

He traveled weekly for business, leaving big gaps of time away from one another—especially for a relatively new connection.

She wanted a good and solid permanent thing—not the forever party that he threw. Would their relationship ever be that?

When she stepped into the bathroom intending to rub lotion on her naked body, she realized the thunder was fading. "Oh, a quick rinse would feel wonderful. And it will clear out any bad mojo in my head."

Twenty minutes later, she plaited her long, dark hair. Willa pulled a simple sundress over her head, the vibrant flowers in the fabric emphasizing the warm, tawny-beige color of her skin. Stepping into flip-flops, she left her apartment with her tiny purse cross-body and her sunglasses dangling from the fingers of her right hand.

"Yeah, I have work to do," she mumbled to herself when a niggling thought about her current painting tried to derail her good mood. "But Damian hasn't stopped talking about his friend for weeks. Gotta go meet the Yankee."

With a grin spread across her face, Willa quickened her step to cover the few blocks to Damian's favorite haunt.

THE CROWD in the Squawking Parrot ballooned with the arrival of the thunderstorm. Some people were soaked, others carried umbrellas; all of them sought protection from the storm. And much to Tim's surprise, most of them seemed to be in good spirits—laughing, chatting, toasting their vacation. The party atmosphere was in full go-mode, and Tim loved it.

With the end of the rain, people drifted to the uncovered deck, reducing the numbers at the bar. When any of them sat at a table, a server appeared from out of nowhere, returning with fresh drinks and menus.

Tim gave up gazing toward the beach and the remaining wisps of sunset, turning around just as an intriguing woman put her arm around Damian's shoulder, and then kissed his lips.

Is this his girlfriend? She's beautiful. Not that he was truly surprised. Damian seemed to have a never-ending supply of attractive women to spend his time with. But there was something different about this one. Something very special. Something that caused his breath to hitch.

"Hey, sugar. There's someone I want you to meet." Damian swiveled around on his stool with the newcomer following. "This is Tim Harley. My old college roommate."

"Hey, who are you calling old?" Tim laughed at Damian, knowing that they were a month apart, with Tim being the younger one.

"Willa, Tim. Tim, Willa."

Tim extended his right hand to the brunette. "It's nice to meet you, Willa." When she wrapped her hands around his, Tim felt a flush of heat pass through every cell in his body. Even though he didn't want to break the connection with her, Tim stood from his stool. "Please, sit."

As Willa made herself comfortable, Tim couldn't help but admire the tan and well-muscled leg that peeked out of a slit that ran nearly to her hip. His fingers twitched with desire to see if her skin was as smooth as it looked. When she turned her head, Tim noticed she had wound her hair tight to the back of her skull, the pattern of the thick, woven strands of black and chestnut pointed to the base of her delicate neck.

"Tim?"

He shook himself from his reverie. "Sorry, did you say something?"

Willa giggled softly while holding a fresh beer in front of him. "Compliments of Damian."

"Thanks." Tim kept his gaze focused on the beverage, bringing the cool edge of the glass to his lips for a deep swallow before clapping Damian on the shoulder. "Thanks, buddy."

"So, tell me about yourself." The smooth cadence of Willa's voice intrigued him. "All I really know is that you two did a bit of hell raising in college."

He chuckled at the reference, mostly because Damian was the party boy. Tim had been pretty studious. But he wouldn't change his friend's story.

"Geez, talk about putting a person on the spot." He took another deep pull from his pint. "Big Irish-Catholic family, mid-sized city with lots of snow and ice for half the year. Not much else."

"Ah, so you're escaping the northern weather." As Willa lifted her glass of white wine, her lips along the rounded rim, the slight purse of her mouth as the beverage coated her taste buds, and the quick dart of her tongue catching the last drop before it ran down the outside of the glass mesmerized Tim.

Down boy!

"Pretty much!" Tim took a step back, forcing himself out of the field of her aura.

"Hey, roomie," Damian's voice was a welcome pull away from Willa's trance.

"What are ya yelling for? I'm standing right behind you."

Damian stood on the rungs of his stool, tipping forward a little too much. Tim laughed at the grandstanding antics of the other man but kept his empty hand aloft in case he lost his balance backward.

"Your glass is almost empty!" Damian shouted for all to hear.

"Yeah, I'm fixing that right now. My turn to buy a round." He nodded his head to Ariel, who was standing across from Damian. "Put your ass back on that stool before you crush her."

Tim pointed to various people to include in the round of drinks. When Ariel raised her eyebrows at him, he gave her a slight nod, raising his own glass and running his index finger across his neck.

Watching everyone get settled in with fresh drinks, Tim put his hand on Damian's shoulder. "Buddy, I'm kind of shot from the drive down today. Gonna take off now."

"Okay. Catch ya soon." When the two shook hands, Tim felt the heat of Willa's gaze. Without stepping closer, he gave her a slight wave and nodded his head before serpentining through the crowd to the front door.

Chapter Two

Tim ambled along the water's edge of Banyan Tree Bay, thinking. Since he had managed to navigate his way out of the fog of grief that had permeated his existence after his wife died, he wasn't interested in crawling back into the darkness. Tim knew he would miss Nikki forever. Some days the loss was more acute than others, but every day it was there. Not unlike a mange-covered feral cat in the backyard. You wanted it to go away, but you knew its life depended upon you.

However, missing her didn't require him giving up his life and live as a shell. A human carcass that still walked, slept, ate, and functioned only in the barest of terms. Fortunately, one of his brothers had stepped in and literally taken things into his own hands. Tim could chuckle now, but there was no humor the day his twin brother, John, cuffed him up the side of the head.

"Hey! This is an intervention." The booming noises of

John's voice and feet filled the nearly empty home in the Pine Hills neighborhood of Albany. "Where are you?"

Tim stayed silent, waiting for him to loop through the entire house before he made his way to the living room. John's heavy boots clomped nearby. Suddenly, the brilliant light of the chandelier pierced through thin spots in the fleece blanket on him and then seconds later, the warmth of his covering was ripped from his grasp.

"What the f—" before the full epithet could leave his lips as he sat up, his left ear was cauliflowered under the crushing weight of his brother's hand.

"Get up!" His assailant grabbed his arm and yanked him to his feet.

"Who do you think you are?" Tim drew his right arm back, ready to break his brother's nose.

"I'm the big brother, remember? And Mom always said it was my job to watch out for you."

Tim flopped back down on the couch. "And what is it you think you need to be watching for?"

John shook his head. "Really? Have you turned on the lights in here lately?" He moved in circles, pointing to various piles of stuff Tim had allowed to accumulate. "And this?" He held the fleece blanket at arm's length. "What the hell died in this? It smells worse than an old black bear when it comes outta hibernation."

"Ya know what John? Go fuck yourself. I don't recall asking for your opinion." Tim vaulted off the couch, intentionally slamming his shoulder into his brother's as he left the room.

"It's been over eighteen months, Tim. Ya gotta get your life back in order." John trailed after him.

"That life's over, bro." Tim found great satisfaction in slamming the heavy wooden door of the half bath in his twin's face.

There was no hiding in the Harley family, and he knew better than to let the silence on the other side of the door fool him. When he entered the kitchen, the deep aroma of a fresh pot of coffee and the sight of his cop-turned-farmer brother with his hat on backward and his arms in a dishpan full of bubbles greeted him.

Tim crossed the room as quietly as possible and placed his hand on John's shoulder. "Thanks, man."

"Don't worry, bud. We'll find that smile of yours again."

For the first time since ovarian cancer had taken Nikki from him, Tim felt the warm glow of optimism as he stared into the eyes of his identical twin brother, who was older by one minute.

MORNING SUNLIGHT BATHED THE WARM, white sand beaches under his feet. From what he'd seen in the past few days, blankets, towels, heavy canvas umbrellas, and countless bodies of all shapes and sizes would cover much of the freshly raked surface by ten a.m., despite the predicted July heat. The idea of "cooling off" in the Gulf waves made him laugh. To his northern born-and-bred feet, it felt as if he were splashing along in the world's largest bathtub.

When he reached the edge of the public beach, or as he had already started calling it, the Bay, he turned around. Carrying a sandal in each hand, he strode with purpose until he found the first side street that led from the beach to the main thoroughfare, Beachside Promenade.

Tim made use of the public shower before sliding into his Teva Terras and making his way up the short alley-like lane. As he gazed at each of the storefront windows through the heavy steel gates, the cop in him wondered about the local crime rate. In his research, none of the statistics had shown a high rate of breaking and entering as a problem.

Looking up, he scanned the utility poles and soffits of the buildings, unable to find a single camera. *Wait, why is there only one streetlight? And it's all the way down there at the busy end.* Tim furrowed his brow about the logic used by the city planners. *Why put it on the end next to the Promenade? That place will be filled with people as the sun goes down.* He still couldn't rationalize their decision but would look for more situations of this throughout the city. Afterall, part of his job was to prevent crime.

"See something interesting?" A sultry, yet familiar, chuckle interrupted his gawking.

"Oh, hey." Tim crossed the quiet street to where she stood. "You're Damian's girlfriend. Willa? Right?" He offered his hand in greeting.

When she took his hand with her much smaller one,

he was surprised by the instant warm flush that filled his groin.

"Are you casing the joint?" She pointed to where he'd been looking upward.

"Um, no. Probably more like the opposite."

"We could play fifty questions here, but don't need to. What were you so interested in?" The leggy beauty flipped an exceptionally long braid over her shoulder just before perching her hands on her hips.

Wow! Where did that hair come from? Was it that long the other night? Tim tried not to raise his eyebrows in response.

Clearly, she expected a straight answer. Now.

"Honestly, I was a little surprised at the steel gates covering the fronts through here." Tim waved his hand toward the beach. "I was wondering why there weren't any municipal overhead lights or cameras."

"Ha!"

Tim tried to decide whether Willa questioned his motives or was about to give him a lecture.

"The city council considers this the low-rent district. Especially since that monster up the block was built."

Sparks flew from the golden highlights in her enchanting deep greenish-brown eyes. *Ooh, she's a feisty one.* "So, not a fan of progress I assume."

"Nope, I love progress. Better than half of my business is done online. But when an overwhelming majority of the townspeople turn out to express disdain for wiping out a full block of our history to make way for towering concrete, but every person on the council votes yes for it? That's some stinky fish heads you got in that bucket. Ya know?" Willa slid a small pouch around her wrist as she spoke.

"I'll take your word for it." Tim caught a flash of sunlight from the gold key she now held.

"Damian never said how long you'd be visiting for." Even though Willa was speaking to him, she leaned to her left to look down the main street.

"Oh, it'll be a while. I came here for work."

She brought her head around quickly. "What field are you in?" Her head cocked sideways.

"Semi disciplinarian, semi head cook and bottle washer. Also known as law enforcement." He watched her closely but saw no change in her features.

"You're the new chief of police." An arch of her right eyebrow followed her matter-of-fact tone.

"Not quite. I don't start for two more weeks." Tim slipped his hands into the pockets of his beige khakis.

"Does Damian know?"

"I'm not sure. He knows I'm here for a new job. And he knows what I did back home. He's smart enough to put the pieces together." He waited for her retort, but she simply stared at him. "Is there a reason why Damian should object to my job?"

Her deep, sensual laugh filled the space between them.

For a moment, as the warm, luxurious sound wrapped around him, Tim nearly forgot that this woman was involved with his friend. *Down killer.* Unfortunately, his groin was still thinking about what her touch had felt like. Adding a seductive laugh to the already attractive package was causing him trouble.

"I thought you two were friends. Like close friends."

"We were, in college. That was twenty years ago. Lots can change in two decades, you know." Nikki's face instantly flashed in Tim's mind before he shook himself back to the present.

"Yeah. Just saying this, but you might want to keep that in mind if you're going to be living here."

"I guess I should talk to him about it today. Can you give me directions to his office?" Tim caught a flash of emotion as it crossed her well-tanned face.

"I'd suggest you try his after-hours location." With her face pointed down, Willa looked up at him from under the thickest eyelashes he'd seen without any trace of makeup.

"Ah, the Naughty Parrot?"

This time her laughter was mocking, not deeply sensuous. "Oh boy. I see you're in need of a geography lesson before you start that new job."

She placed a hand on his bare arm, as if to soften her tease.

Little did she know that anything she'd said disappeared from his mind the instant he felt her fingers squeeze his arm.

"The Nauti Parrot, as in nautical, is in Fort Myers, with a second location in North Fort Myers. The closest of the two is about sixty miles north of here." She looked up at him but still had not moved her hand. "However, the Squawking Parrot is about four blocks south of here on the Promenade."

Willa winked at him as she slowly pulled her hand from his arm and started to walk along the still-quiet side street.

"Hey, wait. Where do you work?"

She pointed over his head, causing him to turn to find affixed to the building a two-foot by two-foot sign with a pastel green background and gold filigree letters crisply outlined in black: Banyan Tree Fine Arts. "You're a painter?"

"No, chief. I'm an artist."

Within seconds, her shapely derriere retreated behind a thick wooden door hanging on massive brass hinges. The deep thud of it closing punctuated her last words.

Chapter Three

"Painter my ass." Willa stomped across the wide plank floor of her home. "Good looking yes, but such a neanderthal. Even Damian had the class to know the difference."

Willa stripped off her exercise clothing, still mumbling about Tim's rudeness. *Wow, it's going to be a steamy one today. Find something very lightweight and flowy after your shower.* When she stepped into the cascading water, happy she had not set the handle at full heat, she let the disgruntled thoughts about Tim wash down the drain along with the sheen of perspiration that covered her body.

Turning her back to the lightly pricking water flow, Willa pressed her hands to the wall of the opposite end. Arching her back, she closed her eyes as the needle points of water massaged her tired muscles. Not only had she increased her exercise routine in the past two weeks, but she'd spent many hours working on the apartment above the building next door. A purchase she'd made on a whim, just to maintain her privacy.

As a middle child, she had spent many years with no space to claim as her own. Twenty-five years later, traces of that tended to creep in totally unannounced. Hence her snap decision to purchase the adjoining building. And even though money was not an issue, she found herself driven to clear out, clean up, and remodel the apartment just in case she needed to rent it out for income. Except, she had yet to convince herself that she'd be comfortable with someone living so close to her.

Once dried off and dressed, Willa found her thoughts floating back to her earlier conversation with Tim. "Ha, painter!"

After doing her undergrad work at Yale, where they had less than a five percent acceptance rate, and then the full ride offered to the Royal College of Art in London, she didn't react well to someone referring to her as "just a painter."

"GUESS I HIT A NERVE THERE," Tim mumbled to himself as he traveled the few blocks south to his temporary dwelling. Much to his surprise, he felt the tickling streams of sweat running down his back as he pulled open the door to the inviting lobby of the Pink Flamingo.

And pink it was. Varying shades of the color blended with large green palm leaves in the wallpaper, accented by black surfaces of tables and what most people traditionally thought of as "the front desk."

"Good morning, Chief Harley." A woman in her late fifties smiled at him from where she sat behind the desk. "What can I do for you?"

Tim leaned against the nearly four-foot-high counter that separated them, tipping his head in greeting. "Good morning, Vera. How are you this fine July morning?"

The older woman's ample bosom jiggled softly as her laughter filled the room. "Apparently, I'm a bit cooler than y'all are. Were you trying to exercise in this weather?"

In the full wall mirror behind her, Tim could see the saturated marks on the chest and underarms of his navy-blue T-shirt. "Not really. Just out browsing."

"Oh, is that what y'all Yankees call looking for troublemakers? I like that you're keeping our streets safe."

Tim chuckled as her Southern voice dropped an octave on her question.

"Now Vera, you know I don't take over for two more weeks." He teasingly shook his right index finger at her. "Don't be spreading rumors about me."

"Oh darlin', with those dimples, ain't nobody gonna believe you're up to mischief. Besides, you do remember who my baby brother is, right?"

Tim realized he enjoyed the innocent and fun conversation with his temporary landlady when he heard the bell on the main door jingle, announcing the entrance of someone else.

"Hey, glad I caught you here." He felt the squeeze of Damian's hand on his shoulder. "I heard you were looking for me." His friend's voice was a combination of the distinctive clip of Long Island and the warmth of the south.

"Wow, news travels fast around this town." Tim looked at Damian's face but was unable to make eye contact since the other man seemed to be more interested in the layout of the aged motel office.

"Well, you know, technology and all." Damian's robust laugh filled the room. "Actually, I managed to catch Willa before she locked herself in her art studio for the day. She told me you were looking for me. What's up?"

Tim nodded, still waiting for Damian to look him in the eye. "Are you busy right now?" His question answered by Damian's mouth twisting in what Tim believed was deep thought. Of course, as a cop, he suspected that his friend was weighing his options of how to answer.

Turning to Vera, Tim pulled his scrutiny from his friend's face. "I will be back in an hour or so to finish our conversation." He directed a coquettish wink and his fifty-thousand-watt smile to the motel owner.

Before she could say anything in response, Tim spun

around and placed a firm grip on Damian's shoulder. "Come on, buddy. I'm hungry, and I'm buying.

Not giving the other man a chance to decline, Tim nudged him toward the heavy glass door he had just come through. As a warm blanket of humid air slapped his body, Tim stepped into place beside his friend.

"Where are we headed?" Damian's hands were deep in the pockets of his lightweight shorts, causing his shoulders to slump.

"I thought I saw an old Howard Johnson's down this way."

Damian's robust laughter took Tim by surprise. "No, that place closed a few years back. But what you did see, is the Hoe Hoe, Joe. Same color, same interior, different menu, better food."

"Better food? How could you beat Howard Johnson's?" Tim was laughing at his friend's facial expressions as he pulled open the heavy glass door of the restaurant.

"Okay, let me rephrase that. Food more suited to the islands than their traditional menu was."

Once seated at a corner table away from other customers, Tim resumed their conversation as he watched Damian carefully place his sunglasses on the table. "Seriously, I've got to tell you that news really does travel fast around this town."

"Ha. Willa did say it was important." Damian kept his head down as he spoke.

Tim wanted to be angry with the attractive brunette,

but just the mention of her name gave him a surge in his lower abdomen. She probably knew he planned on sussing out Damian's attitude before bringing up the job he would start soon. "Well, yeah. But not like 'get here immediately' important. I haven't seen you in a few days. Time to catch up a little without a lot of other people around to distract us."

"Catch up? What have we been doing?" Damian's raspy laugh led Tim to assume the other man had been out late the previous night at one of his forbidden poker games where he was able to smoke with abandon.

Was that narrow-minded? Maybe, but the state smoking law in Florida prevented him from doing that inside of a bar. Also, many of Tim's thoughts came from his time as a child, when he often heard his mother or maternal grandmother refer to a raspy voice as a smoker's voice. And heaven forbid you should hear it come from a woman's mouth before, or after, Sunday morning mass. Reflecting back, the older Catholic women in his life were tough ladies.

Tim found himself chuckling at the memory, causing Damian to tilt his head. "Was it something I said?"

"Oh, sorry, no. Just one of those old-fashioned things my grandmother used to say. You may remember that the Irish are fond of tossing about idioms."

"Yeah. And they frequently confuse me."

Watching a smile cross Damian's unshaven face, Tim looked to his right to see a lithesome brunette approaching the table. "Good morning, gentlemen. I'm Xaviera and I'm here to serve you this morning."

Sparkling green eyes winked at Damian before turning their focus to him. Tim could barely contain a barking laugh when he realized the restaurant name was Hoe Hoe, Joe, and their server's first name was the same as the author of the book *The Happy Hooker,* and she directly said, "I'm here to serve you."

Damn Uncle Patrick. His father's brother had been only too happy to drop the book into Tim's lap as a birthday present the year Tim and John turned sixteen. It had not escaped Tim's notice that the book looked well used with its many dog-eared pages.

"Good morning, Xaviera." He inclined his head in her direction.

"How about I get you guys some coffee while you take a look at these?" She placed a pair of plastic-enclosed menus on the table.

"Please." Tim's nose twitched at the slight smell of bleach that hung in the air since the lists of food options arrived. *Better that than the putrid stench of a dirty dish cloth.* He never understood why any food establishment allowed staff to "clean" tables and menus with a heavy cotton cloth carried around in a bucket of gray, soap-less, and fetid-smelling water.

"Lots of fish on here."

"Yup. Some folks eat it three meals a day. Not unlike cattlemen in the west and avid deer big game hunters in the north. For the most part it's local, not complicated, and usually a great price." Damian tapped his finger on the lower, right-hand corner of the menu. "This is probably what you're looking for."

Glancing down the list, Tim smiled at the sight of a picture of buckwheat pancakes with sunny-side-up eggs.

"But remember something, you will not find real maple syrup here." Damian winked at him from under a lock of blonde hair.

"Apparently I will have to train my taste buds or cook my own breakfast."

Once Xaviera returned with their coffee, Tim asked for scrambled eggs, bacon, and rye toast while his friend ordered a bowl of grits with fruit on the side. When they were alone again, Tim cast his eyes around the restaurant to determine who might be sitting close enough to hear what he was about to say. Resting his hands to either side of his half-empty coffee cup, he looked across the table.

"Damian, where abouts is your office?"

The unkempt blonde locks bounced as a deep laugh rose from the other man. "Office?" Running his left hand through his curls, Damian finally looked Tim in the eye. "I'm self-employed. Why would I need an office?"

"You know, for your things. Like a desk or computer. Maybe a desk for your receptionist? Some place cool to meet with clients? Why wouldn't you want an office?" Tim couldn't help but shake his head and hold his hands out, palms upward, to Damian.

"For Christ's sake, Harley. When did you become

such an old man?" Damian pushed back from the table, tipping his chair on the back legs.

With his untamed, bleached blonde hair and his loud print shirt, Tim thought he looked like a punk. "I'm not an old man. Just a responsible one. And clearly, you're a sensitive one." He stopped speaking when he saw Xaviera approaching with their food.

"Is there anything else I can get for you, before you fall on your ass?" She had one tilted eyebrow directed at Damian.

"I'm curious about something." Tim waited as she took her focus off the faux surfer sitting across from him. "Is Xaviera your given name?"

"Why would you question it?" She slipped a fat pen in her cleavage and cocked her right hip, causing her miniscule cutoffs to slide higher as Tim chuckled.

"Just stringing a few things together here. The restaurant is named Hoe, which is slang for whore. When you introduced yourself, you said you were here to serve us, and your name is the same as the real-life author who penned *The Happy Hooker*. That's either a super-sized dose of coincidence or a clever marketing ploy that few customers appreciate."

"I'll tell you what, handsome," Xaviera gave the dark curls on Tim's head a quick finger massage, "you come back next Saturday and maybe I'll give you an answer." She rolled her neck and well-tanned shoulders for a moment, causing her generous bustline to expand before his eyes, before bending down to peck his cheek. Then the flirtatious server slipped the check into his shirt pocket and gently lifted his chin, insinuating that his jaw was gaping. “You can pay your bill at the door on your way out.”

Tim ignored Damian’s laughter and ate his rapidly chilling breakfast.

Chapter Four

"I can't believe you got us tossed outta there." Damian wiggled his hands in front of him.

"Oh, quit it. If they wanted us to leave, we wouldn't have been given the time to finish our food and get refills on our coffee."

"Do me a favor," Damian had stopped walking.

Tim turned around. "What?"

"Don't cause trouble when I'm around. I don't need that shit following me."

Trying not to laugh at his friend, Tim decided it was time for their chat. "Hey, you see that cut across to the beach?" He pointed across the street. "Let's go that way. At least we'll get a little breeze from the water."

Neither man spoke until they reached the wave line in the nearly pristine, white sand. Tim noted how few people had set up areas on the beach. He thought there would be a crowd by that time of day.

"Do you know why I moved down here?"

"Not really. I assumed you wanted to escape the memories after your wife died." Damian pushed his hands deeper into his front pockets, causing his shoulders to slump. "I mean, we got lotsa hot women in this town. No relationship needed for a good time."

Tim wondered how deeply involved Damian and Willa really were. "Nope. I'd have to abandon a whole lotta people to get away from my history. Nikki also grew up in Albany. We met in high school." Tim followed a lone sea gull as it floated on an unseen current of air.

"Did I mention that Ariel has been asking about you? She says you're hot in a pasty-white skin kind of way."

Tim chuckled at the back-handed compliment but let it drop. "Hey, stop for a moment, will ya?"

Damian came to a halt, positioning himself so the morning sun was behind him. Sliding his sunglasses into his hair he looked at Tim. "What?"

"I'm here for a new job that I haven't told you about."

He watched his friend straighten his shoulders and take a step backward. "What's that?"

"Chief of police."

Tim saw the flash in Damian's eyes as the three words sunk in. "Wait. You came to my paradise to bust people and rough 'em up?" His unshaven jaw flexed.

"What do you think I've been doing for almost twenty years?"

"I knew you were with the cops, but I thought you were some sort of tech guru."

"Yeah, I was for about two years, but the whole time I

was sitting in a crime analyst's position. So, I took exams and worked my way up. You'd be surprised how much I learned as a keyboard jockey. The department knowledge I learned while writing programs for them came in handy and made me a valuable candidate."

"I 'spose it didn't hurt to have your brother pulling strings for you." Damian openly smirked.

"If you're talking about John, he worked for the State Troopers, not the Albany PD."

"So, you came all the way down here to bust folks for going barefoot in restaurants? Or nude sunbathing? Why would you give up the power and money you had there?"

Damian had taken a few more steps backward and slid his sunglasses into place, thoroughly blocking Tim's vision of his eyes. But Tim witnessed enough in the other man's defensive body posture to know he was hiding something.

"And I thought you'd welcome me with open arms. Did our friendship slip somewhere along the way?"

"No, man. I think you might be a little off in the head for taking an inside desk job, that's all." Tim saw Damian's shoulders relax slightly, but he kept his eyes covered.

"It only has to be, as you call it, an inside job, if I want it to be. But once I'm fully comfortable with my knowledge of Banyan Tree Bay, it's possible I will take advantage of the air conditioning more often than not."

"When do you start?"

"End of the month."

Damian surprised Tim when he stepped forward, giving him a hearty one-armed hug. “Congratulations, buddy. And welcome to town as a permanent resident. Can I buy you a drink?”

Tim pulled his cell from his back pocket. “Thanks, but it’s only ten thirty. I think I’ll go catch a hot shower instead.”

“Well, stop by the Squawking Parrot later today. I gotta get you drunk before you go all strait-laced cop on me.”

“Sure thing.” Tim laughed and shook his head as the two parted ways, thinking about how many failed marriages he’d seen amongst his Albany coworkers, most of those caused by alcohol.

THE SIGHT of Willa walking toward him on the Promenade, her long gams wrapped in sheer, billowy pant legs, was an unexpected surprise for Tim. Based upon the grin he felt on his face, pleasantly surprised was a far more accurate description. He held up his right hand in greeting, appreciating that she quickly pulled her sunglasses down and let them rest on her chest, held in place by a lime green Croakie.

“Where are you off to this fine afternoon?”

The very slight dimple on her right cheek deepened as her smile increased. Hooking her thumb over her shoulder, Willa dropped her smile for a moment. “I told Damian I would meet him for lunch at the Parrot.”

"Lunch? We didn't get around to breakfast until ten."

She shrugged her well-defined shoulders at him. "Yeah, so? When he suggests we share a mealtime, he drinks, and I have food."

Tim couldn't control his right eyebrow from arching with opinion. "What a life. Drinking at lunch when you're not on vacation. It must have something to do with living in paradise."

"Or being an alcoholic." Willa placed her hands on her hips and pursed her captivating lips as she gave a slight shake of her head. "And what about you?"

"Nope, not a heavy drinker."

She bent backward, casting a raucous laugh to the sky.

"Was it something I said?"

"More like something I didn't say. What I meant was, where are you heading to? In pants?"

"What's wrong with pants?" Even though he intended it as a serious question, a naked picture of Willa popped into his mind for a second, leaving him with a pair of crowded khakis and a warm flush on his cheeks.

Willa pointed to a large digital clock–thermometer mounted on the bank a few buildings down the street. "You're in southwest Florida in late summer. Most people wear shorts."

"Ha! You have pants on. Besides, I'm going into the station for a meeting with the current chief. Color me old fashioned but my professional comfort zone won't let me do shorts right now. Once I'm settled, maybe." She lifted the Croakie and sunglasses over her head and slid them into what seemed to be a pocket in the diaphanous fabric.

Grasping the thin material in her fingertips, Willa spun in a small circle, much to the delight of a few passersby. “I’ll have you know that these are Thai pants. A gift from my cousin.”

She ran her hand across her abdomen and down her thigh, barely grazing the shimmering gold and green material. Watching her, his fingertips could practically feel the gauzy fabric of the outfit she wore.

Instead of reaching out, he slid his twitchy hands into his pockets.

“Listen, I gotta go. He might be retiring, but I don’t want to keep Chief Jones waiting. After our meeting I thought I would take a formal tour of this fair city.”

“Stop by my studio after you change outta those pants and I’ll take you for a ride.” Willa grinned on one side as she winked at him. A moment later, she walked away, shouting something over her shoulder.

Tim thought it sounded like “not pants” but he couldn’t be sure. In all honesty, his mind was stuck on her suggestive offer.

Breathe deeply, Harley. You’re about to meet the ultimate Deputy Dawg and you don’t need to be sporting a hard on.

WILLA TRIED to focus on Damian's face across the table because the noisy lunchtime crowd made it difficult to hear him. At first, by the way he rested his face in the palm of his left hand, fingers splayed across his lips, she thought Damian was hung over. When she realized that he was intentionally obscuring what he said, she pulled his free hand toward her.

"I can't hear you. Speak up." She felt like she was shouting over the three-thousandth rendition of Jimmy Buffet's Margaritaville. Some days she wished more bars played pure instrumental Caribbean music instead of popular, trendy songs despite the following the artist had.

"Maybe I don't want anyone else to know what I'm saying." The mulish look Damian cast at her wasn't helping her state of mind. His earlier text insinuated that the conversation was extremely urgent, so she had given up the unspoiled afternoon light streaming across her studio to meet him. With the unpredictable nature of what the summer heat did to Gulf weather, pure blue skies were a gift from the painting gods.

"Get over here," she growled through gritted teeth, "Now." When he slid into the booth, his thigh pressing up against hers, her anger fizzled. "Thank you. Now what were you saying?"

Damian drew in a deep sigh. "When you told me to find Tim, you knew. Didn't you?"

"Knew what?" She placed her hand under his chin, pulling his face around so she could see his eyes.

"Don't play with me, Willa."

"What are you asking, Damian? Did I know he was a cop?" She leaned as far away from him as the booth would allow. "Yeah, I did. And that's why I said you should speak to him. So you would know."

"Why did it matter to you if I knew my college buddy was now a cop?" His blue eyes had turned to ice as he grabbed her hand. "You think I'm up to no good?"

Something in Willa's belly clenched as she felt the spittle of his angry words on her face. She'd known him six months, and not once had she seen him angry. Damian was always the affable guy—the beach-bum-esque perennial man child, and all who met him, loved him. The fun partner that loved to dance and snuggle. The one who filled her carnal needs. The one she was considering spending the rest of her life with. *Wait. Where did that come from? Just a few hours ago you made plans with his buddy.*

Very slowly, she slid her hand from his grasp. "What are you talking about?"

"I want to know why you thought I needed to be aware of who the new chief of police will be. And I want the truth."

Willa considered excusing herself to use the ladies' room, freeing herself from the literal trap she found herself in. She looked over his shoulder, taking in the waves crashing to shore, leaving a sparkling trail of water racing back into the Gulf. *I gave up an afternoon of painting for this bullshit?*

When her gaze returned and found him wearing a smirk, Willa's temper torpedoed. "So it's the truth you want?" She slapped his perfect pecs with both hands, pushing him back in the seat. "You made it sound like time was of the essence for this discussion. As I was concerned for your welfare, I closed my studio for the afternoon. Yeah, that studio. The one where I make a very comfortable living creating stunning paintings that people want to decorate their homes with."

She dropped her voice an octave, a sign of how deep her anger flowed. "I don't think you're up to something. I know you are. No visible means of employment, we never spend time at your place, hushed phone calls that you leave my side for—but you've always got cash when it's time to party with peeps."

An inscrutable mask had covered his face, but she wasn't cowed.

"While extremely sexy, and incredibly irresistible in bed, you are either: one, a married man; two, working undercover for a three-lettered agency; three, in witness protection; or four, a dealer of some sort." She pushed against his muscular arm. "Now let me up. I have work to do."

Damian stood to let her leave the booth just as a server arrived with the salad she expected to have for lunch. After the young man left, Damian returned to sitting. "Stay away from Tim."

"What? You think you tell me what to do?" Willa leaned next to his ear. Not giving him the chance to answer, she pushed blonde wisps aside affording free access to run her tongue down the outer rim and then dance on the tender inside, teasing him into an audible groan before biting the tender lobe.

"Ouch. You bitch!" He yelled at her and reached for her hand.

She taunted him outside his grasp. "Don't you ever again make the mistake of thinking that you control me." Willa watched the storm clouds pass through his eyes several times, but she knew he wouldn't hurt her. This was the first time either of them had shown anger toward the other, and she wanted to be sure that he never forgot how volatile hers could be.

"I'm just saying that I don't want you near him unless I'm there too." He spoke slowly and softly, apparently choosing his words carefully.

Not fooled by the change in his voice, Willa cupped his chin as she lifted the plate full of salad, oozing with blue cheese dressing, and dumped it in his lap. "Not a fucking chance." Pulling a wadded-up twenty from her bikini top, she dropped it on the table and left him sputtering through the putrid scent of the dressing she knew he detested.

Chapter Five

It was well after four in the afternoon when Willa escorted Tim across her studio, stopping only to unlock an enormous steel door.

"The easiest way to get around town is on two wheels. And speaking for myself, I'm really not into the whole tandem bike thing in this heat."

He watched her wave an imaginary fan near her face before holding one finger in front of her. Moments later, he looked at a black helmet she tossed to him.

"Safety first." She tapped the red one she was pulling on.

"What are these for?" Tim cast his gaze around the well-organized space. "All I see are boxes."

Willa grabbed his hand, sending an unexpected bolt of desire to his balls, and led him through a small opening he hadn't even noticed.

Sharp investigative skills there, Harley. On the other side he found a gleaming black motorcycle. The sleek structure hinted at the ability for extreme speed. A smile toyed with the edges of his lips.

He feasted his eyes upon a Moto Guzzi V9 in person for the first time in his life; it was the gem of Italian heritage, and he couldn't help but touch it. His fingertips lightly caressed the eagle emblem on the gas tank, his hands mere inches from Willa's thigh, his pulse increasing as he envisioned applying the same sexy touch to her. As if she'd read his mind, Willa gave his hand a quick, light tap, pushing it away.

After backing the bike off the rack that protected its tires, Willa straddled the frame. Tim admired her strength while handling the motorcycle, wondering why he hadn't seen this coming. She was definitely a take-charge kind of woman, and this mode of transportation certainly suited her.

She raised her hand over the top of her helmet, triggering a motor to whir as a small overhead door clicked and began to rise.

Willa slowly moved the bike to the curb with the late afternoon sun glinting off the polished black paint and chrome. "Well, are you coming or not?"

Even though he couldn't see the sass in her eyes through the dark screen of her helmet, there was no mistaking it in her voice. He tugged the headgear into place and moved quickly through the exit, filling the seat behind her as the heavy door clunked to the ground, with the sound of a lock sliding into place.

"Any requests for what to see?"

The lilt of her voice filled his helmet, briefly surprising him.

Even though he had ridden motorcycles for years himself, he hadn't done much upgrading in his equipment. Fresh air and silence were his favorite companions when riding—not listening to music or another person.

"You're the driver. I'm at your mercy." He stretched his arms out to either side, laughing. But as soon as he felt the click of Willa putting the bike into gear, he was happy to squeeze his thighs to hers and wrap his arms around her abdomen to steady himself. He just hoped the erection that kept showing up to wave hello whenever he was around her wouldn't take this opportunity to become familiar with her attractive derriere.

"Open road it is." After looking in both directions, she pulled away from the curb, crossed the promenade, and continued down a narrow street Tim had yet to walk. Swiveling his head from side to side, he assessed the conditions, discovering another area where the city leaders had failed to install lighting or cameras. But the owners had steel bars like the ones Willa and her neighbors had installed.

A few minutes later, their travel speed increased quickly as she pulled onto the freeway. For the first mile, they remained in the far-right lane. But once the traffic thinned a little, Willa showed impressive driving skills, crossing in and out of the other lanes but still being courteous to fellow drivers. It didn't take long before she moved back to the right and exited the main road. With a few quick changes of direction, they pulled into a small park facing the open water of the Gulf.

As soon as Willa killed the engine, Tim stood from the bike, giving her a few feet of space to dismount—and him a nice view to watch her.

Her denim-clad legs circled the motorcycle as she flipped a few switches and pocketed the keys in her light-weight leather jacket. Pulling off her candy-apple red helmet, she shook her head, causing a long, thick braid to bounce from side to side.

"There's a great set of rocks right over there." She pointed to a clump of trees. "We'll have some shade."

Tim waited a moment to see if she would leave the helmet on the bike or carry it. Even though they had the beach to themselves, they might not have a clear view of the motorcycle. Stepping beside her, he opted to carry his. Afterall, it wasn't his to lose.

After pulling off her coat, Willa surprised him by bending at the waist, grabbing the hem of her jeans on her left ankle, and pulling a zipper all the way to her hip. The quick clicking sound that released her long, tan leg mesmerized him. Without explanation, she repeated the action on the right and then unbuckled the waistline. She shook out what were essentially chaps and folded them into a small pile.

"Look at your face!" Willa laughed boldly as she reached to touch his chin. "You thought I was stripping, didn't you?" She patted a lightweight pair of shorts and settled on the large, smooth rock next to him. "You might be an attractive man, future Chief Harley, but I do have more class than taking you the first time we're somewhere sort of private."

Tim felt his eyebrows arch well into his forehead at her boldness. The woman was, as his father and uncles used to say, a pistol. Ignoring the compliment, he answered the question. "No, I didn't think you were stripping."

"Ha. I call bullshit." With more laughing, she bumped against the length of his torso. "So tell me, what makes you so easy to tease? Is it the innocence of a northerner or the Catholic schoolboy?"

"How did you know I was a Catholic?" He turned to look at her, the gold flecks in her brownish-green eyes threatening to distract him.

"Damian mentioned something about how many Irish were Catholic, which morphed into there being a ton of cops in the New York City area who were Irish. Like generations of them."

"Nice theory, but I grew up in Albany—about one hundred and fifty miles north of the city."

Willa pursed her lips in response.

"And what makes you think I'm easy to tease?"

"Oh please." She stroked his right cheek. "Your skin is still flushed from watching me step out of that denim."

Tim really wanted to stand up and put some much-needed distance between them, but he knew he would embarrass himself with the erection filling his shorts. Instead, he changed the subject. "So where are we?"

"The locals call this Isla del Sol Tenue or Island of the Fading Sun—" she pointed to the horizon "because it faces the west."

"That's too logical." He chuckled at the simplicity but loved the enchanting sound of her speaking Spanish.

"You will discover that the locals have many sayings and practices rooted in American Indian, Spanish, and Caribbean culture. A melting pot, if you will."

Just when he felt it was safe to stand, Willa blessed him with a warm smile. *What am I doing out here with this gorgeous woman?*

"Have you lived here long?" *Surely idle chat was safer than...what? What do you think you've been doing? Seriously, how long has it been since a woman smiled at you?* He wanted to laugh at himself but was afraid Willa would take it personally.

"We moved here when I was a child."

"From?"

"Thailand."

"Oh, really. Did you have family there?"

"Sort of." With her chin slightly lifted, she stared at the water." "My mom was Thai, but my dad was American. They met when he was in the service. You know the deal—he swept her off her tiny little Asian feet." She laughed at her own poke at people assuming all Asians were tiny.

"They're both gone now?" Tim surprised himself at how soft his voice came out.

"Yeah. But it's a long story. Me and my sibs carry on

the Davidson craziness." Willa tipped her head and smiled at him. "How about you? Lots of family? I mean, that's what they say about you Irish-Catholics, right?"

Tim guffawed at her generalization of his heritage. "Well, actually, it's pretty accurate for my family." He slid forward on the rock until his feet touched the sand. Toeing off his boat shoes, he grounded himself by burrowing his dawgs into the cooling grains.

"There are five of us. Four boys and our baby sister, Mary Kate." He looked up when he heard Willa's giggle. "Right, her name is so very Irish."

"Well, I suppose it is—especially if you watch John Wayne movies. What about your brothers?"

"Besides me, there's John, Liam, and Patrick. So, at least two of those go with the whole culture thing."

"I believe yours does also, Timothy. Is it all right if I call you that?" She had gotten off the rock and gone about three feet toward the water when she turned back with her question.

"Oh, jeez. Does that mean I'm an Irish punchline?" He intentionally pushed his hands deep into his pockets to assume the shrug of a younger man.

"So, my new friend, I would say that your dark locks, and nauseatingly beautiful eyelashes that sweep to a peppering of tiny freckles may have given you away even if your name was Fred." She waved him to her side. "How about a short walk in the water to give the after-work traffic a chance to clear up, then I'll take you to the best fish restaurant in town."

"We're still within the city limits of Banyan Tree Bay?" He looked around at the rural space surrounding them.

"Yeah, we are—but it's mostly forever wild around here."

Without waiting for him, she sprinted to the waves. Her loose-fitting shorts danced at the edge of her well-muscled derriere.

He wasn't sure any of this was a good idea, but he knew it was enjoyable.

FOR WILLA, the afternoon spent with Tim was just the balm her heavy heart needed. Not only was he easy on the eyes, but he was easy to talk to.

With Tim, she faced none of the constant bravado that came with Damian. Everywhere they went, that man was high-fiving and backslapping other men, while kissing the cheeks of women. And always pulling people in to join their table or booth. To Willa, it almost felt like Damian was afraid to be alone with her. But he always took her home and spent the night. Depending on the amount of alcohol he consumed, they would have intense, deeply satisfying sex. But some nights he landed on her bed and started snoring immediately, leaving her with over two hundred pounds of very loud company and no choice but to sleep on her own couch.

She knew it was unwise to compare the two men. Afterall, Tim might also be the same type of drinking beefcake who could benefit from the use of a CPAP machine. Though something told her he wasn't. But she needed to be more honest with herself. Did she truly enjoy the time with Tim? Or was she, if only in her own head, getting back at Damian?

The more she thought, the less inclined she was to relax with a book or watch television. For years she had used exercise as a diversion. A way to tamp down any anxiety. Part of her would love a late run, but there had been rumors of abductions around the Bay area, and the women never returned. Given how many hours of sunlight were available each day, it seemed daft to put herself in harm's way by going out so late. Instead, she trotted to her bedroom, peeled off her clothing, and slid a sleeveless caftan over her naked body.

Over the years she had worn many different outfits while working in her studio. Running shorts and tank tops, bralettes and bike shorts, full leggings and an old button-up shirt of her father's. But tonight, she felt sexy. And the flowing silk material of the dress, as it slid effortlessly over her breasts and around her legs, appealed to her.

Stepping in front of her floor length mirror, Willa admired how her cleavage danced at will in the deep V-neck opening. Her nipples responded to the cool touch of the rich fabric gliding across them, causing an unexpected surge of heat to cross her abdomen and settle in her core.

Remembering the look of desire that she had found in Tim's eyes several times that day, along with the intriguing erection she'd seen him trying to hide, she licked her lips while sliding her right hand under the billowy material. A soft moan escaped her lips as she slipped her fingers into her own moisture. She thought about how solid his thighs were and how easy it would be to wrap her legs around his waist, sliding herself down his shaft. Tim Harley might be the next chief of police, but he was one sexy Irishman.

Somewhere in the back of her mind Willa heard the multiple pings coming from her cell phone as she continued to stroke herself. *Oh, bugger off.* No one knew where she was, or that she was about to come standing up—something she discovered increased the intensity of her orgasm—so she decided to block out the sound. And then the phone began to ring, multiple times, in the annoyingly shrill tone she used when listening to loud music. The one she'd forgotten to turn down when she arrived home earlier.

When the phone fell silent after four rings, Willa took a deep breath, allowing herself to relax and find her rhythm again. Just as she felt the mind-numbing sensation tug at her, a man's deafening yell brought her back to reality.

She shook her head and arched her back. "This better

be a fucking emergency." Her breasts and buttocks jiggled with abandon beneath her dress as she crossed the second story loft and pounded down the set of stairs to the front door. With the incomparable fury of a sexually frustrated woman, she practically tore the door off its hinges to find Damian leaning on the door jam, carrying an open bottle of liquor.

When the blonde-haired beach bum she'd always found attractive leaned in to kiss her, Willa planted both hands against his chest and shoved with everything she had, causing him to stumble backward into the quiet street.

"Not now, Damian. Just go away."

After screeching at him, she slammed the heavy wooden door as hard as she could, flipped off the outside light, and threw all three locks—including the deadbolt she usually ignored. "Stupid bastard."

This time when she returned to the sanctuary of her home, Willa tossed back a double shot of Pusser's Rum, draped her caftan over the chair in her boudoir, and slipped between the soft, clean sheets of her king-sized bed with a rabbit vibrator in her hand. No doubt, Willa was intent upon regaining what Damian had just stolen from her—the very vivid picture of Tim's body joining with her own, if only in her head.

Chapter Six

Two weeks flew by quickly for Tim, due in part to spending time with a certain long-haired beauty. After dinner the day they had explored Isla del Sol Tenue, he insisted she take his personal cell number. Each day since then, there had been a reason for her to call or text him.

As he stepped from the shower, he heard his phone ping on the table of his suite at the Pink Flamingo. Other than his brother John or sister-in-law Kara, Willa was the only person he expected to message.

Taking a moment to dry off and then wrap the towel around his waist, he picked up the phone, pressed his right thumb on the screen and laughed. Three texts and the most recent one was from Willa.

> Time to saddle up, chief. The posse's waiting for you at the jail.

He still wasn't sure why she made frequent references to the days of *Gunsmoke* and *The Wild Wild West.* Maybe because he'd told her stories about his sister-in-law having horses and what a tenderfoot John turned out to be; she thought people from the north were all cowboys.

With an absurd picture of Albany in the days of the horse and buggy flashing through his mind, Tim moved on to encouraging messages from his brother and his brother's wife. They were a good couple, best friends, co-workers, and parents thrown together for a bad reason: the death of Kara's first husband. Almost five years later, it was difficult to find them apart for more than a few hours. Tim sent a separate thank you text to each of them.

Lowering himself to the couch, he scanned through recent notes from Willa, laughing at some, puzzling over others. She was dating his friend. But in his experience, neither partner in a good relationship was open to the attention of another person. When you're in love with your 'person,' you don't flirt with others, even in a light fashion.

The tiny numbers in the upper left-hand corner of his phone surprised him. He had less than forty-five minutes to shave, finish dressing, grab some coffee from the reception area, and walk the six blocks to the police station. Fingers crossed Vera had other hotel guests to wait on when he reached the lobby so she didn't detain him with chat.

WITHIN SECONDS after she sent a supportive text to the new chief of police, Willa thought she heard a soft knocking on her front door. *Who could be here so early?* She waited a moment for the picture from the security camera to pop up on her phone. Damian. *It's six-fifteen. Did he stay up all night?*

Unlike days in the past six months, the sight of him didn't excite her. And she knew she'd been avoiding him. They'd grown distant in the past few weeks—only getting together when he invited her to join him at the Squawking Parrot. And he hadn't suggested so much as a morsel of food since she'd dropped the salad in his lap. Willa wasn't even sure if they were still a couple...or if she wanted to be one.

When curiosity got the better of her, she trotted down the steps to open the door.

"Hey." His eyes looked clear, and his face was clean shaven.

"Hey yourself. Whatcha doing here?" Willa folded her arms across her sweaty bosom, unconcerned about the moisture from the early run she'd taken through the peaceful streets of Banyan Tree Bay.

"Can we talk?" Damian pointed up the stairs behind her.

"About what?"

Noise on the Promenade caused them both to look in that direction for a moment.

"A few things."

Her stomach dropped when Damian looked her straight in the eye. He never did that.

"Please?"

"Okay." She turned to climb the stairs. "Lock that behind you, please."

When she'd taken two steps, the bolt of the lock fell into place with a *thud*. Before she was halfway up the staircase, Damian's large body was behind her. Many times, when they had climbed these steps together, he had playfully cupped her bottom or raised her dress up and taken little nips at her flesh. The thought of such intimacy with him made Willa dash to the top, leaving Damian to raise his face to hers, one eyebrow lifted in question.

"You okay?"

"Sure, why wouldn't I be?" She shrugged her shoulders with nonchalance. "I'm still charged from my run, that's all." Nothing could be further from the truth. If she came clean with him, she would say that she was exhausted, and she'd much rather be in the shower loosening up her muscles than socializing with him. She held open the next door, her waved hand giving him permission to enter her private space.

By some rote of past experience, he sat at the island that filled her kitchen while she stood between the other side of it and the sink. Leaning against the counter, she raised her cup of coffee in the air. “Can I get you some?”

“Thanks, but no. Already had three cups. Ice water would be nice, though.”

Willa grabbed a slim clear glass from the cabinet, pressed it against the dispenser on the fridge and then slid it across the marble surface toward him once it was full. When she raised her own beverage to her lips, the now-cold coffee coated her tongue with cool, bitter bean water. But rather than being overly dramatic, she swallowed quickly and refilled the cup with fresh brew.

She looked at Damian, his shoulders slightly slumped, his head tilted down. His breathing was so shallow that for a second, she thought he was sleeping. *It’s showtime.*

“Damian, what did you need to see me about so early in the day?” Willa tilted her head in question.

“I miss you.” He dropped the unexpected bomb onto the literal and figurative island between them. “I know I screwed up.” His head rose slowly, his expressive eyes searching her face. “What can I do to make it up to you?”

Even though she heard his words, they sounded hollow. “You could start with an apology.” Willa set her cup on the counter behind her, then stood straighter, her feet planted apart in a defensive pose, arms akimbo.

“I just did.” The softness she’d just seen in his features quickly vanished. “What else do you want from me?”

“You know what, Damian? I’m not asking you for

anything. Never have, never will." She started to pace. "But you insulted the hell out of me."

"Me? You dumped a fucking plate of food into my lap. How do you think I felt when people in the restaurant were laughing at me?"

His response literally stopped her in her tracks. "You have no idea why I'm angry, do you."

"No, I don't."

"I have an early business appointment so I'm not going to play twenty questions with you." Heat flushed Willa's torso and crept up her neck, a sure sign she was ready to explode. Taking a deep breath, she stared at the countenance she'd always found to be sexy in a playboy sort of way. He'd recently had his blonde hair trimmed, taking away the curls she preferred. His full, very kiss-able, lips defied the Anglo-Saxon heritage he claimed. After what seemed like several minutes, she finished her thought. "You insinuated that I would be unfaithful to you. That I couldn't be trusted around your friend." She waved her hand in the space between them. "That I had something to hide."

She took eight steps in the narrow space of her kitchen before turning to him. "You treat me like I am a call girl. You never consider what my schedule is. What my business needs. Whether or not I'd like to do things with my friends. And you never take me to your place. Do I embarrass you? Or are you married?"

Damian leaned back in the seat of the stool where he

perched, as if he were afraid of her striking him with a long board.

"Can I say something now?"

Resisting the urge to spew more of her mental injuries at him, Willa nodded.

"You know, I just might have things to hide."

Her eyes bulged at his admission.

"No, nothing bad—like illegal bad. And no, I'm not married."

"Then what are you trying to say?" Her patience waned.

"What I'm saying is that me," he ran his hands down his chest. "This? This is all bluster. I got nothing other than my looks. After college my parents tried to pull me into line, you know, save my life and all of that because I had already pissed through a crap-ton of money. I had some great jobs up north, ones that paid me six figures, but I was bored." He traced the veins in the marble with his right index finger. "All the run-around buddies I had in high school and college were settling down, including Tim Harley. I didn't see much of him because he didn't like to overnight away from his sweetheart."

Willa tried not to wince at his use of air quotes around the word sweetheart when he referenced his college roommate. She didn't want to think about the women Tim had held in his arms. "What about you. Didn't you have anyone special by then?"

"Had is more like it. But she dumped me."

"Don't tell me. You treated her badly, never picked up

the check, always slept at her place, or left after sex?" She focused her eyes on the surface of the island. "How many others were there?"

"Jeez Willa, you make me sound like a total loser." He shook his head and held his hands in front of him. "I'm not. Yeah, there were more after that. But I never tried to hurt any of them."

"Damian, you're over forty now. You walk around in flip-flops, cutoff shorts, and those stupid T-shirts styled like the ones most older men use as underwear." More criticisms filled her head. "I could say more, but I'm sure you're already aware of them."

"Maybe, maybe not. I'm sorry I hurt your feelings, Willa. I trust you. I don't think you'd cheat on me."

She was still undecided when he stood up and stepped around the large island she'd kept between them. The scent from his body filled her nose, stirring up memories of their intimacies. In a feeble protest, she kept her arms at her sides when he pulled her to him. Against her better judgment, Willa leaned her head against his chest, encouraging him to wrap her in the strength of his arms. But as soon as he lowered his head to kiss her, Willa jerked free of his hold.

"No. We're not doing this today." She held her hand out when she saw him advance in her direction. "You don't get that sort of easy pass anymore."

"But we're good together baby. Makeup sex is always the best." He dangled his talented tongue from his mouth. "I'm so hungry for you."

"Well maybe that's part of the problem for me. We've been together a long time for this to just be sex. Maybe I want you to make love to me. Cherish me. Treat me with respect, in the daylight, out in public. Not just when we're here, hidden from all eyes."

"What are you saying?" Gone was the tenderness he showed earlier. Instead, his usual snarky grin had fallen into place.

"What I'm saying is that you'll have to work on your sales pitch before we'll be intimate again." She walked to the door, turning the knob and pushed it open. "Out."

Damian stalked from the kitchen, his feet pounding heavily across the hardwood. He stopped in front of Willa, grasping her fingers and raising them to his lips. "I don't know what's gotten into you lately, but this is crazy. I just apologized. What do you want from me?"

Ripping her hands away from him, she tilted her head toward the opening. "Now."

Willa leaned against the closed door, waiting to hear the lock of the bottom one fall into place before she let out her breath. Thinking about how close she had just come to giving him full permission to use her for his own satisfaction, she started to shake.

But throwing him out felt great. It was just the shot of strength she needed for her soul. And now, she had every intention of satisfying her lady parts in the shower.

Chapter Seven

Tim felt the tension drain from his shoulders the moment he walked through the front door of the station. Once signed in at the front desk, he moseyed along the wide hallway leading to the chief's office. The heels of his leather shoes clicked slowly, pausing when he stopped to read a poster, job openings, and various fund-raising efforts. Tim nodded and smiled at people he passed, greeted the few he met on his two previous visits. In his heart, he hoped this department would have a solid core that respected the community at large but also took care of its officers. And if he didn't find one, he would rally with his co-workers and create it.

What began as a slow-moving morning took an about face when Tim's administrative assistant tapped on his door and then stepped in. "Chief, the commissioner and the former chief would like to see you."

Discreetly, Tim placed his left index finger on the

passage he was reading so that he would not lose his place. "When?"

The cheeks of the slender young man flushed quickly. "Now, sir."

Tim drew in a deep breath, holding it a moment before exhaling. "Thank you, Adrian. Did they say where?"

"Yes, sir. In the commissioner's office, in city hall." Adrian slipped out quietly while Tim put a paperclip on the section of the manual he'd been reading. "Ugh, day one and politics already."

Tim grabbed his sports coat, pulling the office door closed behind him. "Thanks Adrian." He waved to the young man, click-clacking his way back through the main hall and out into the morning sun. By the time he reached city hall just two blocks away, Tim wished he had dressed in some form of wicking material rather than all the cotton he wore.

Minutes upon entering the building, a staff member escorted him to a palatial office on the second floor. It took a serious dose of self-discipline to keep his thoughts from showing on his face. In Albany, the second floor of the capital was dedicated to the governor and their staff. The population of Banyan Tree Bay was very similar to Albany—a little over ninety-five thousand—with a comparable sized police force of five hundred. How did the commissioner score such a nice set up, and on the second floor?

With polite handshakes all around, Tim sat in the leather chair offered to him, the natural material stretching to accommodate his weight.

"Tim, welcome to the Banyan Tree Bay Police Department." The large man across the desk from him inclined his head at the end of his greeting. "I would love to tell you that you should expect a few weeks to settle in, take your time getting to know some of the force and the civilians working there."

"But?"

"Former Chief Jones has brought some interesting rumors to my attention this morning. Howard, would you please bring Tim up to date?"

How long should I expect the former chief to keep running the office?

"Some of the people I know on the water have seen an increase in the drug cargo coming into a few of our ports."

Tim sat up straighter in his chair. *Get over the hows and whys of him having this info and just use it. If he's doing this to screw you over on your first day, karma will take care of him.*

"Did they say which ones?" He turned to look at Howard's face.

"Yes. Banner and Lucia."

"Hhm, two different types of port. Any indications on the sort of vessels the mules are using?"

The former chief took a deep breath. "Lucia is definitely using the lighter pleasure crafts, but Banner is looking like it's the ferries."

"Howard," the commissioner jumped in, "which islands are we talking about?"

"Saint Thomas, Virgin Gorda, Dominica, and an uninhabited one that's part of the Little Sisters."

"So, a few in the BVI and one in US territory. At minimum, we'll need the DEA for some of this. Tim, what are your thoughts?"

"With all due respect sir, I don't think the BTBPD needs to handle international drug smuggling beyond what comes into our ports. For anything in US waters, I'm sure the Coast Guard will handle that."

Tim hoped he didn't sound lazy or out of his element but heading up an international drug ring was going to need a whole lot more resources and muscle than they had there in Banyan Tree Bay.

"I want you two to work out a schedule of surveillance without putting our officers in harm's way. Keep track of the chatter and let's see what we can come up with in the way of background. In the meantime, I will alert the mayor. Once we have something concrete, I'm sure she'll take it to the governor." The commissioner paused a moment. "Howard, I can cover your expenses as a contractor, but Tim is in charge."

When the commissioner stood, Howard and Tim did also. Clearly, they were dismissed. Once they stood on the expansive sidewalk in front of city hall, Howard spoke up.

"I retired because I had run out of steam for juggling all of the chief's responsibilities. So, believe me, I'm not trying to step on your toes here. I don't know how much drug trade you had up north, but we have a lot since we sit on this open coastline." He pointed in the general direction of the bay. "With twenty miles of it in your jurisdiction, the topic of this meeting with the commissioner will become a regular occurrence just because of smuggling—drugs and other pricey things." He seemed distracted by two men walking on the sidewalk across the street.

Tim bit his lip when he realized that one of them was Damian.

"Anyway, have your pretty administrative assistant with his pink hair give me a call when you're ready to start work on this." Howard let out a belly shaking laugh after his disrespectful comment about Adrian, reminding Tim of the depiction of Boss Hogg, a fictional Southern law man up to no good.

AROUND FOUR O'CLOCK, Tim felt the vibrating signal of his personal cell phone indicating an incoming text. Reminding himself that he was the head of the department, and it was okay to check it, a surprised smile filled his face when he saw Willa's name.

Hey. How about a first day meal after work?

LOL, sure. What time?

5, Black Caesar Pirate Park, near the koi pond. Bring paper towels with you.

Tim answered with a thumbs up emoji and returned the phone to its clip. *Maybe we're having a picnic? It's bloody hot out for that.* He guffawed at himself. Such a Yankee. People have lived in southwest Florida for generations without a little bit of outdoor time killing them.

Resisting the urge to swing by the Pink Flamingo to get his Jeep, Tim pulled on the baseball cap he'd brought into the station earlier. The humidity hadn't released its hold despite the time closing in on five o'clock. In the north, thunderstorms tended to break this sort of weather, but not here. One had rolled through shortly after he returned from the meeting with the commissioner and having lunch—but, he swore it was harder to breathe now.

"Hey, you chose it. As the saying goes, quit yer bitchin'." Laughing loudly to himself, Tim noticed the nearly abandoned sidewalk leading to the park entrance. Which pretty much made sense. He assumed people were either home for dinner, avoiding the heat, or both.

A straight run of macadam led him to a gap in the vegetation with a dirt foot path leading to their meeting place. Having visited the park over the weekend with Willa, he knew the tranquility of the koi pond appealed to her. And he agreed. The closer he was to the manufactured oasis, the more he smiled, looking forward to private time with his new friend.

"Hey, you." Willa stood from a long bamboo bench, stretching her arms around his neck and pecking his cheek. "I'd like you to meet my friend, Jenn. I've told you about her."

Tim was a little surprised to find that Willa had brought a third person. Since her text an hour before, he'd had trouble concentrating on anything other than her. In a short period of time, the sight of Willa's beautiful eyes and smile had become his favorite thing to see in Banyan Tree Bay. And even though he was disappointed by this development, he extended his right hand to the woman on the seat. "Hi. Willa's told me a lot about you."

"Jeez, all good I hope." Her inviting smile contradicted the nervous tone of her voice.

"Yup." Tim waved to the cluster of fish milling in the water about six feet away. "Hey, those guys look ready to eat. What's your plan?" He directed his question to Willa.

Without speaking, she pointed through the trees toward a vendor cart parked on the main trail of the park. Tim felt it his body flush when her gaze returned to his face. "Not every meal has to be five star. But honestly, these really are great hot dogs. Right Jenn?"

Willa had already started walking toward the stainless-steel rig. "I'll bet you didn't know she had a secret love for everyday food, did you?"

Tim looked at Jenn's powder blue eyes that also had

specks of chestnut, admiring the sparkle of humor he found there.

"I grew up in a family of five. Hot dogs were a weekly staple in our house." He laughed as her eyes grew larger. "My mom's favorite way to serve them was in Kraft Dinner."

"What's that?" She cocked her head, causing a blonde streak of long bangs to fall sideways.

"Kraft Dinner?"

She nodded her head.

"Elbow macaroni and dehydrated orange cheddar cheese. It came in a box—you cooked the macs and then added butter, a splash of milk, and the packet of cheese while the noodles were still hot. We considered it a delicacy. Especially when she cut the dogs into one-inch pieces and threw them in. And, somedays she'd swap out the dogs for canned tuna fish."

Jenn looked a bit queasy by the time they caught up to Willa.

"All right, chief. I thought we'd celebrate your first day in low-key, humble, yet delicious, fashion. My personal favorite is this one," Willa pointed to a picture hanging from the side of the cart of a plain hot dog on a bun with a thin line of yellow mustard. "Obviously the usual line of condiments are available, in addition to a pretty good coney sauce. What's your choice?"

Tim faced the vendor, a middle-aged woman with a pile of curly red hair on the top of her head, held in place by a loose net. "I'll have two of these," he pointed to the picture of a hot dog adorned with a single line of ketchup, riding in a bun. "Along with a bag of chips and a Pepsi. But first, please serve these lovely ladies."

The tan skin of the woman wrinkled as a smile covered her face. "Ladies?"

Willa opted for one dog on a bun with mustard and an iced tea, while Jenn had two plain dogs in the paper dish, no rolls or condiments, and a bottle of water. Before Willa could argue money with him, Tim pulled thirty bucks from his front pocket and gave it to the vendor. After that, all three made their way back to the bamboo bench.

"To your first day on the job. May they all be safe and boring." Willa held her iced tea in salute.

"Agreed." Jenn tapped her bottle to the edge of each of theirs.

The morning meeting with the commissioner flashed through his mind but he wasn't comfortable sharing details. "Thank you for those kind words. But I'd like a little excitement. Living in paradise is already multiple layers quieter than any given day in Albany."

All three smiled and dove into their dinner. The trickling sound of the running water rushing over intentionally placed rocks and waterfalls pushed out any sounds that came from the street and lulled Tim into feeling like they were somewhere in the Caribbean.

An hour later, after easy banter about living in an island paradise, the three of them left the park to go their separate ways. Walking back to his room, Tim tried not to let the density of his day take away from the calm he'd found by the koi pond. A few yards from the Pink Flamingo, Tim heard Willa calling him. He turned around to find her trotting across the Promenade toward him.

"Hey. Did I leave something behind?" He cocked his head at her.

"Um, not that I know of. But I have a question." She paused until he nodded at her. "How's your apartment hunt going?"

"Ha, not very well. I think Vera's trying to rig it so no one will rent to me, and I'll be her tenant forever." He laughed at his own joke. "Why?"

"I know this may seem crazy, but why not rent the extra apartment I have?" He saw her look down at the sidewalk, not meeting his eyes.

"What? Where?"

"Shortly before you arrived, I purchased the building adjoining my own. It's taken me a while to get the apartment spruced up and furnished. But it's available if you'd be interested."

Tim couldn't believe what he was hearing but he liked it. "Sure. Did you say furnished?"

"I did. It may be a bit too feminine for you, but you can change the paint and furniture if you want to. I'm heading there now if you'd like to see it."

"I'd love to." Tim gestured for Willa to turn so they were heading back north along the main street. If he wasn't careful, she'd see the very happy grin on his face.

She might be Damian's girlfriend, but Tim loved spending time with her. Not only was she physically stunning, but she was also intelligent and challenging—two characteristics he found very attractive. Walking beside her for the few blocks, Tim felt like the luckiest man on earth.

Chapter Eight

Willa was as surprised as Tim when she blurted out the words, "Why not rent the extra apartment I have?" She had intended to sound more blasé about it, kind of work her way into the suggestion.

She almost stopped in mid-step when it dawned on her that he might think she was coming on to him. *Gack! Now what?* Then her dastardly logical side chimed in. *Are you? Are you interested in him? You do think he's hawt, hawt, hawt!* Since when did the voice in her head mimic a giggling teenager? *That's right, even though his tan isn't much, he is one sexy snowbird. And you've been fantasizing about him while using your love stick. But wait. Hello, you have a boyfriend. And Damian is this guy's friend. Are you crazy?*

As they approached the front door to the apartment, Willa squelched the internal guilt session in her head. Pulling the key from her pocket, she opened the door. "You go on up and look around. I'll wait down here."

"Okay, sure."

His brow wrinkled but she couldn't determine whether he was angry or confused.

Closing the door behind him, Willa took to pacing back and forth in front of her buildings. When she thought of it that way, she couldn't suppress the smile filling her face. *My buildings.* "Yeah kid," as her dad used to say, "'you done good kid.'" She missed her parents. The sadness of her mom's long ago passing was a dull ache, deep in her chest. But her father's was still so recent that just thinking of him brought a sheen of emotion to her eyes.

After about five minutes, she heard Tim coming down the stairs. With a grin on his face, he stepped to her side, offering his hand. "Deal."

"But you don't know how much the rent is. Or whether utilities are included." Willa knew her jaw hung open, but she couldn't believe he'd made a decision so quickly.

"I don't care. You are a decent human with a good heart: this is a great place to live and it's an easy walk to the water. What's there to quibble about?"

"I may have rushed this a bit." Her cheeks filled with heat at the admission.

"And what's that supposed to mean? Was this just a tease to see if I liked pastel walls and geometric rugs?" His broad laugh wrapped around her as if he had pulled her into his arms, teasing a similar sound from her chest.

"No, I mean that I haven't figured out a price yet."

"Since I have been shopping for a few weeks now, let me help you with this. Second floor, ocean front flat, two bed, one bath, full kitchen and living room. I say 2400 dollars." His eyes never left her face. "Or I can be your maintenance man for 1800 dollars."

Thinking about how much she had spent on contractors for the work she couldn't handle herself, whether it was time, strength, or knowledge impeding her, Willa knew this was a good deal. "You know how to swing a hammer?"

"Whoa. Just so you know, unless you're working on demo, hammers have pretty much been replaced by screw guns. If you're gonna hang with the maintenance guy, you need to bone up on the lingo." Tim teasingly bumped her shoulder with his.

"Then I think we do have a deal. Do you want a contract or just month to month, like a gentleman's agreement?"

"Either is fine with me. When can I move in?"

Willa found his grin to be infectious. Slipping the key into his hand, the warmth of his flesh traveled through her entire body, leaving a smile on her face and a pulsing need in her mound. "Anytime you'd like."

"I will give Vera the news when I get back there. But I'd like to wrap up the week with her, especially since I've already paid for the room. I'm sure she would refund it to me, but I see no reason to burn a bridge in my new town."

"I'm changing into some form of swimming gear.

Care to join me on the beach?" She saw him look down at his long pants and boat shoes.

"Yes, in about half an hour. Hopefully I can catch her now and then get changed." He pointed down the single lane street that ended at the white sand of Banyan Tree Bay. "I'll catch up with you out there."

Willa nodded and watched him walk away jauntily. As soon as he turned the corner, she sprinted to her own door, punched in the security code, and raced up the steps to get ready.

"AREN'T you just a ray of sunshine. Was your first day that good?" Vera practically purred at him when he entered the lobby of the Pink Flamingo.

"Hello, Vera." Tim leaned over the desk to pick up her hand, placing a chaste kiss on her knuckles. "You are exactly the person I was looking for."

"Oookay, but first ya'll have to tell me about day numero uno." Her southern voice drew out a few words and clipped others.

"The good news is that I'm still employed." He laughed as her eyes widened into a surprised look. "Seriously, Vera. When I walked in the station this morning, I wasn't sure about this change in my career, my life, and in this monster relocation to humidity hell." Tim pulled the front of his shirt out to exaggerate how hot he was. "However, I have discovered that the job will be exciting. And I will be benefitting from your brother's vast knowledge for at least a few weeks."

"Oh, Howie's a good boy." She pushed her hand to give Tim a modest aw-shucks gesture.

"Vera, I do have other news. I have found an apartment to rent." He was pleased her face lit up with excitement.

"Oh, that is good news—for both of us."

"How so for you? I planned on staying the remainder of this week so that you don't lose the business."

"Oh honey, you're welcome to stay as long as you want, but don't you worry your handsome little head about me. In all honesty, I've been giving you the friends and family discount to make your transition easier and to get my brother outta that chief's chair before he has a stroke. Don't worry, the next person to lay down on that king-size bed will be paying a premium to see the ocean."

"Oh, you are a businesswoman to the core. I sure am glad I already had a peek into the soft heart of Vera Mattice." He watched her fingers fly across the keyboard on her desk, the long acrylic nails she wore making a distinctive click with each strike.

"You're paid through Friday night, with a Saturday morning checkout. Are you planning on being here that long?"

"Yes, ma'am. Unless you need me out now."

"Nope. It'll give staff the long weekend to clean the place," she held her hand up in front of him. "Not that I'm saying you're dirty or anything. But my staff tends to move a bit slower on the weekends than the ones here Monday through Friday. I'll list it as available starting Tuesday."

"Now, I would be honored if you would have dinner with me tomorrow night."

As her cheeks flushed a delicate pink, Vera bowed her head a second. "Why that would be lovely."

"Great. With that settled, I am going to change into beach garb and catch the sunset while cooling off."

Tim had no intention of mentioning his date with Willa. *Date?* Yeah, it was. No way the excitement running through him was just about his successful first day on the job.

WILLA DECIDED on a quick rinse in the shower before pulling on a solid blue tankini and swim-skort. In her mind, a bikini shouted, "look at these magnificent melons of mine" and that was not the message she wanted to convey to Tim.

Crossing the sand with a large, floppy-brimmed hat holding her braid, and carrying a towel with multi-colored stripes, the sound of the waves wrapped Willa in a blanket of peace. As the day's heat arose from the hot, glittering crystals of what the locals called sugar sand, she was quite thankful she had worn thick rubber-bottomed walking sandals instead of flip-flops. Reaching the water's edge, Willa pulled out her phone to text Tim a suggestion about foot gear. But when she unlocked the screen, she found six new texts from Damian, and her mood plummeted.

Dropping her towel on the dry sand, she worked her way through all of the messages.

I miss you.

I need you in my life.

Please Willa, don't cut me off anymore.

Please, can you answer me?

I've got an idea, lets take a catamaran cruise this weekend, just you and me. We can make it to the Caribbean in one day if we leave early.

Please.

Crap. Why doesn't he leave me alone?

Willa didn't know what to think about how to answer him, especially as countless questions tumbled around in her brain.

"Something serious?"

The sound of Tim's vibrato startled her. Giving the

phone an anxious squeeze to change the screen to black so he wouldn't see Damian's begging, she turned to face him. "Nope, all's good." Willa pointed to his feet. "Glad to see you didn't wear flip-flops. The sand will all but melt them on a day like this."

His gentle chuckle calmed her nerves. "They're not for me. Not only do I hate having something between my toes, but I think they look like crap. Too much casual vibe."

Willa wrapped her arms around her torso, laughing loudly at his statements. "Wow, seriously stuffed shirt. Did you hear yourself?"

"Um, yeah. Just telling the truth. Flip-flops make me crazy because nobody picks up their feet. They're always like *scuff-scuff* everywhere they walk. I want to boot them in the ass and yell at them 'pick up your feet.' The nuns in my school would have lifted them up by an ear for that lazy stride."

The more he talked, the harder it was for her to breathe. Finally, she held her hand up. "Stop, before I die." She watched his brow furrow in question. "Before you say that secret brain nugget about flip-flops to another person down here, please remember that you have moved to southwest Florida. Most of us have six pairs of sandals or flip-flops for every pair of shoes in our closet. And about a hundred miles from here, you can scoot through the Keys and head out to the Caribbean. There's lots of sand and lots of water. Flip-flops are considered respectable footwear around here."

"Yeah, maybe if you're rinsing off in a public shower." His soft mumble was barely intelligible. "Well, so are my Tevas." He raised his leg, wiggling his foot in front of her. "And mine peel off pretty easily, see?"

Within seconds he was barefoot and walking into the warm summer water of the Gulf. Willa followed suit post haste to step by his side.

"Wow, I might have to take a real dip. This feels fabulous." She looked up at his eyes, their warm, azure depths nearly hidden by the shadow of the porkpie hat he wore. "But first, I need to get this phone out of my pocket."

"No dry bag?" He pulled out his cell, fully encased in a thick layer of plastic.

"Never even thought of it. You keeping yours with you or shall I put it under my towel?"

He appeared to mull it over for a second and then handed it to her.

"I'll be right back."

But before she could turn, she felt Tim's hand on her arm, searing his own personal brand into her skin. Looking up to see his face, she was dazed to find his torso bare and him holding the shirt out to her.

"Please take this for me."

As the next small wave came in, she nearly tripped in the shallow water when his request ended with a smile.

"Uh, sure." Wrapping both of his items into her grasp, Willa dashed to the shore, splashing the water as high as her buttocks.

Oh, what are you doing here? He's almost naked. Did you not see those pecs with black hair leading down to his chest of family jewels? Damian says he wants to make up with you. Do you care about that? Wouldn't you rather have Tim?

She stood for a moment, taking a deep breath to steady herself before turning around. Striding through the bath-like water, she kept her focus down until she heard a splash. Looking up, she saw Tim's feet disappear under the surf. Wondering about his ability to swim, she stood still, waiting for him to re-surface. In moments, he shot up out of the ocean, blowing water from his mouth and wiping his jet-black hair back from his face. His masculine chest glistened in the late sun as water streamed through the thick hair covering his pecs.

Holy hubba, hubba. Damian will have to wait until tomorrow. Or maybe forever.

Without a second thought, Willa dove into the waves to meet Tim.

Chapter Nine

Tuesday had come and gone, and the Wednesday morning sun shone high in the sky before Willa reached out to Damian.

> Hey. Sorry for the delay. Been crazy busy around here.

But Willa saw no reason to wait around for him to reply. In her experience with Damian, he was rarely up before nine. And since she didn't like wasting daylight, she slipped the phone into the side pocket of her favorite harem pants and set out for a blistering walk to the art supply store on the north end of the Promenade. Many of the materials she used shipped directly to her door. But in the last few days, she'd felt an interesting joy that she wanted to express. A joy that was begging her for new colors of paint. And Willa didn't want to trust the sample pallets she used online.

Having covered the eight blocks in record time, she

arrived at the store at the same moment the door was being unlocked. The owner, Sari, waved happily at her through the glass as the security gate lumbered up. When the opening was clear, she pushed the front door outward and pulled Willa into a strong hug.

"Girl, how are you?" Her voice, with its Island intonation, warmed something deep within Willa.

"I am well, Sari. How about you?" The very unique scents of oil paints, chalks, pastels, acrylics, and cleaning agents reached her nose. Drawing in a deep breath, Willa felt her body relax in the familiar environment.

"I can see that you are. There's happiness all over your face." Sari pulled Willa with her to the checkout area to allow two other customers access to the door. "And I am well, also. Thank you for asking. But it's been a few months since you have come to see me. To what do I owe this lovely surprise visit? You know I could ship anything you want to order, right? I've even been known to hand deliver."

"Yes, I do. But I woke up this morning with sunshine in my heart and felt the urge to pick out some new colors in person." She shrugged her shoulders and smiled. "I have a new painting filling my brain and I just need to get it out of me." Willa spread her arms high and wide with an explosive burst, "Voilà! Like that, I want the world to see it hanging in my studio, in all of its acrylic glory, marked with an NFS. You know, not for sale!"

"Oh, but why won't you sell it?" Sari's eyes opened wide with surprise, the clean white in stark contrast to her dark skin. "Mommi, do you have something to tell me? Or maybe someone to tell me about?"

"No, my friend. I'm just happy." Willa smiled broadly, hoping there wouldn't be any more questions. She wasn't ready to share her heart with anyone, not even Sari. "Now, I need to choose some new paint and get back home before I lose the best light of the day."

STEPPING BACK from the glistening canvas she had worked on most of the day, Willa jumped at the sound of a knock on her door. Using a heavily stained cotton cloth she kept draped on the paint tray of her easel, she finished wiping her hands before she picked up her phone and checked the security camera. *Damian.* That's when she noticed many missed texts from him. And a few from Tim. She trotted down the stairs to the door, flipped the inside locks, and opened it.

"Are you okay?" Damian reached out to touch her, but Willa inclined her body away from him, avoiding his touch, and the expected smell of alcohol. "I haven't been able to get in touch with you all day."

Shrugging sheepishly, Willa gave him a slight grin. "Sorry, been in the zone all day so my phone was shut off."

"Can we talk?"

Willa started to invite him in and then remembered the painting she'd just been working on. There was no way to mistake the distinctive cheekbones, or the stunning blue eyes of Tim. No way did she want to risk him seeing it. She leaned heavily across the door jam, hoping to fill the opening as much as possible. “Oh, sorry, place is a mess. Haven’t cleaned in days.” She scrunched up her face and shook her head. “How about I meet you somewhere?”

Damian shot backward a few feet, leaning his shoulders away and sliding his hands into his pockets, looking like she’d just slapped him. “Yeah, I guess that’s okay. What time?”

“Give me half an hour. Meet at the Parrot?”

“Nah,” he shook his head, causing his blonde hair to slide across his forehead. “How about the beach in front of the new place?”

“Okay, see you then.” Willa closed the door quickly before the many questions in her head popped out of her mouth. Damian’s demeanor was totally out of character, starting with the fact that he appeared to be stone cold sober, and it gave her chills. Rubbing the goose bumps peppering her arms, she raced upstairs and locked the next door behind her.

A FEW DOZEN feet from the mega-hotel, Willa took the old ipe wood plank walkway to the beach. Her mind traveled back a year to the public hearings preceding the approval of the building plans. On the blueprints, the architect proposed demolition of the forty-year-old wooden path leading from the concrete sidewalk halfway across the sand to the demarcation for high tide. But the locals howled vehemently about losing the herringbone patterns of now silver Brazilian hardwood expected to last another thirty-five years. The outcry was so robust that in the end, the architect not only left the walkway, but also added ipe wood to the design of the rear exterior walls and the raised deck seating area for the restaurant.

As she stepped into the sand, she caught sight of Damian near the water's edge. Facing the bay, with his shoulders slumped, he looked defeated. A posture she'd never seen from him. With her steps near silent against the perpetual crashing of the ocean, Willa reached his side without his knowledge.

"Hi."

Damian jumped in surprise when she touched his arm. "Oh, it's you." He canted his head toward her. "Hi."

"Expecting someone else?" A nervous giggle escaped her lips, while her gaze searched his face.

"No, no. Just thinking." He turned inland and pointed to a concrete bench above the high tide mark. "Shall we sit?"

Willa nodded and dug her feet in with each footfall. Falling into place beside him, she was able to keep up with his long-legged stride. When they reached their intended seat, Damian dropped himself down near the middle. Nervous from the odd silence, Willa left a gap between them and rotated so she could see his face.

After a few moments, he took the lead without

looking at her when he spoke. “I know I screwed up badly. I never meant to treat you like that.”

She waited a second to see if he would make eye contact with her, but he didn’t.

“Damian, look at me.” Willa struggled to keep her hands folded in her lap since her natural inclination was to reach out, to calm him by touching his tan arm. After a few long breaths, he turned his face toward her, leaving the rest of him pointed at the water.

Burying the urge to analyze his posture, Willa forged ahead. “Do you even know why I was upset?”

“Um, because we don’t spend enough time together?”

Willa felt her eyes squint but held her tongue. Damian was the one leading the interaction and he needed to resolve the problem, not her.

“I don’t know. Maybe you want me to do more chick things with you. Like go to the movies, shopping at the mall, or get dressed up and eat in bougie restaurants?”

“Those things would be nice, but they’re not exactly my style. And the fact that you don’t know that is why we’re here.” She saw a flash cross his eyes. “You don’t know me very well. All of our time is spent in a bar environment, with your friends. And when we are alone, we’re in the sack, doing high-octane things. But as soon as you are satisfied, you conk out and never get up in the morning with me.”

Willa stood from the bench, crossing the sand a few feet before facing him.

With his elbows resting on his thighs, and his head drooped, the only thing he seemed to be interested in was the cooling sand.

"To be very blunt, you make me feel cheap. Like I'm a whore."

Damian's head snapped up, flipping his hair away from his eyes. Their blue depths turning to ice as he shouted. "What is that supposed to mean?"

"I am half Thai, Damian." She walked a few feet before turning back to him. "You throw money on bars and tables and then shout over the music in some half-assed pirate voice, calling me your wench, grabbing me by the arm, regardless of what I want. It means we're some sort of ignorant caricature, as if I'm your concubine."

Willa turned her back on him so he couldn't see the tears threatening to spill down her cheeks. She felt the heat from his body just before he slipped his arms around her shoulders, pulling her backward against his solid frame, his erection firm against her derriere.

"Please, listen to me. I'm out of my league with you." His hands slid down her arms, slowly turning her to face him. He nuzzled her cheek and neck until she looked up at him. "I'm just an overgrown frat boy from Long Island. I have had everything handed to me, including women. I've never worked for anything in my life." He kissed her forehead. "In truth, I'm not as smart as you. I'm just a spoiled rich kid asshole."

Despite her misgivings, Willa couldn't help but

giggle at his admission. “And what are you going to do about it?”

“Can we start over?”

Despite seeing the anxiety in his eyes, Willa struggled to commit to him. For many weeks, thoughts of Tim had entertained her. *But you and Dame have a history.* Willa could only nod. Just once.

“Will you take a boat ride with me this weekend? Just you and me?” Damian leaned down, his lips capturing hers with a gentle nibble. Quickly, Willa pushed away from him before his tempting and teasing caused her to let her guard down. “We’ll have hours to do all the talking and getting to know each other that you want.”

“Wait, you know how to captain a boat?”

“Yeah. I actually have a commercial license. What do ya think? We can leave tomorrow and spend Labor Day weekend on the water.”

“Wow, this is a surprise. What about food and water? How do we stock up that quickly?” Lost in the excitement of being away from shore, Willa forgot her own responsibilities. “Oh wait, my store. I can’t close up and leave for a long holiday weekend. It’ll cost me thousands in missed sales.”

“Call your blonde friend, the nurse, to cover. Maybe she’s got time off.”

As he spoke, Willa was already texting Jenn.

Hey, any chance you aren’t working this weekend?

Yup, three days to lay on the beach, trying to eat ice cream before it dribbles all over me since I don't have some hottie to lick it off of me. 😊 Why?

Damian wants to go away for the weekend. Just us, no drinking friends. We really need this. We'll leave tomorrow. Can you cover the store for a few hours each day Friday through Monday?

I thought you guys were on hold.

Yes. But I want to give him another chance. Please?

Sure, but you're going to owe me.

Thx a mill. I'll make it up to you.

Call me later.

Yup.

"Jenn can cover!" Jiggling with excitement, Willa spun in circles, holding her hands high in the air.

It had been so long since she'd been on the open water, listening to the sound of a vessel cutting through the surface, squealing when a rogue wave splashed her sun-soaked skin, falling asleep to the gentle rocking. Not until this moment did she realize how much she missed the considerable time she had spent with her father on their boat.

Damian reached to hold her hand, "I'm so glad you're going with me."

Willa leaned back so she could see Damian's eyes. *Is he already playing with me?* "What do ya mean. You were going anyway?"

"No. Now Willa, hold that temper. I sent you a text a few days ago and made the reservation hoping you'd say yes."

"Oh," she stepped out of his arms, a little embarrassed that she was ready to accuse him of nefarious behavior. "I see." She pointed to the sun as it was about to slip into the ocean. "I have to go pack. Call me with the details tomorrow, okay?"

She gave Damian a quick peck on the cheek and faced the wooden walkway. But before she could move, he grabbed her hand. "This makes me so happy. Thank you for giving me a second chance."

Pulling her hand from his grasp, Willa tapped him on the chest. "Don't blow it surfer dude." She heard him suck in his breath as she walked away, wondering if he realized how precarious his position was in her life.

A few blocks from leaving Damian, Willa's phone vibrated in her hand. Turning it over, she found Jenn's name.

"Hey, thought I was calling you."

"Well, I didn't want you to forget now that you're all distracted and stuff. Did you hit your head on something today?"

"What? Why would you ask that?" Willa felt her defenses getting ready to strike at Jenn.

"Did you not just agree to go away with your ex-boyfriend, Damian?"

"Why are you calling him that?"

"Willa, listen to me. Damian is a user and he's not good for you." Her friend drew a deep breath. "The last few weeks you've put distance between you and him. And you've been happy."

"I just think I should give him another chance." Willa stamped her foot on the sidewalk even though Jenn couldn't see her.

"A second chance at what? Hurting you again? You know who won't hurt you? The chief. He's a good man."

"What the hell, Jenn? Where is this coming from?"

"Because I've been around you two and I see how you look at each other, the way you coquettishly bump shoulders. I know there's potential there."

"Jenn, I ought to just hang up on you. Why are you being disloyal to Damian? Or suggesting that I should be."

"Willa, you're a smart cookie on so many levels. Sometimes I'm even a little jealous of you. But you have totally missed the boat with this guy, Damian. He has no loyalty to you. And as soon as you put the permanent smack down on things, he'll jump into bed with someone else."

"Ya know what, even though I need your help, I don't care what you think right now!" Willa saw the disapproving stares people on the sidewalk gave her as her response to her friend burst from her lips.

"Okay, do it your stubborn-as-a-donkey way. But I'm going on record as saying that the best man for you is Tim Harley. Not Damian, 'the dude with no car' Buck."

Much to Willa's surprise, Jenn severed the call, leaving her to stand gaping at her phone while the crowd of tourists on Beachside Promenade bumped past her.

Chapter Ten

The tumbling nature of Tim's life, since arriving in Banyan Tree Bay, stunned him. And, good or bad, he didn't know where to give credit. Every morning, he rose before six, exercised on the beach while the sun crossed over the buildings on the east, and was showered by seven-thirty. Several times his brother John had called during his run, helping him eat up the miles and time, as well as keeping his mind off the burn in his calves. Even though he'd been a distance runner for years, the pliant surface of the sand was totally new to him, stretching and expanding his legs with each step.

His new job was also responsible for moving time along so easily. With the guidance of the former chief, the BTBPD had gathered evidence that Tim expected to lead to a large drug bust. He found that once tapped into the chatter, detailing plans, mapping out surveillance sites, and identifying the players, all fell into place. It was even possible that in the next few hours he and six detectives would make a sweep of the rental companies at Port Lucia. How much inside info they would dig up was anyone's guess.

Tim moved quickly to the station six blocks away, all the while silently sorting through recon details. When he reached the corner of the promenade where Willa's business was, it dawned on him that they hadn't spoken since the night on the beach, right after he had decided to rent her apartment, over three days ago. Stopping for a moment, he sent her a text, expecting her to be up.

Hey stranger, got plans for lunch?

Oh, hi. Lunch would be nice, but not a long one. Wrapping up some business loose ends then going out of town for a few days.

All pleasure, I hope.

LOL, of course. I'll text you later.

Okay, have a nice morning.

You too, chief.

Tim got a weird, niggling feeling about the text exchange. Willa was a busy career woman, and he knew that she had a personal life with Damian, but he felt like she was pushing him away. And, honestly, he was skeptical about his college-era friend's intentions when it came to her. But no one was asking his opinion. After today's lunch, staying out of their relationship seemed like the gentlemanly thing to do. But first he needed to see her in person to make sure she was okay.

Hi. Running behind. Want to have pizza here for lunch? Is 11 okay for you?

Good idea. Lots of meetings this afternoon to prep for. See you then.

WHEN THE TIMER on his watch chirped at 10:45, Tim practically sprinted from his desk to the street. The six or so blocks to Willa's apartment stood between his empty stomach and food. Not to mention that he was really excited to see her. He tried not to run like a schoolboy, with his necktie flying over his shoulder and the change jingling in his pockets. Even though he forced himself to walk, Tim arrived at her door at the same time as their lunch. Handing the delivery woman two twenties and a big smile. He turned when Willa opened the door before he knocked.

"Perfect timing!" Tim held the pizza box aloft.

The dimple on her face made his heart happy. He leaned forward and kissed her cheek without thinking. Then saw her tongue dart out to wet her lips. *Whoa, more than this pizza in my hands is hot.* Following her upstairs, he realized it was the first time she had invited him into her apartment.

"Nice place." He looked around the open space, taking note of the soft colors and fabrics.

"I've got everything ready over there," she pointed toward the bistro table close to the kitchen.

They ate the first slice in silence. *Is she going alone? Girls' weekend? Something with Damian?*

"So, I think I'll be moving my stuff in this weekend." The few seconds he waited for her to look up and answer him were excruciating.

"Great. I'll bet you'll be happy to have a home instead of a room."

"Yeah. My own music, my own cooking, and a bit more privacy. Unlike walking past Vera a few times each day."

Willa looked at him with a slight purse of her lips as she placed another slice on his plate. She dropped her gaze to the spatula in her hand, moistening her lips again.

I wonder if she knows how much that tongue is killing me?

"So where are you going this weekend?"

"Oh, just a couple of days away with a friend."

"I see." Willa's answer sounded vague, but at least she didn't say Damian was part of her plans.

"Ya know, just some downtime to recoup from summer traffic."

She sounds a little off. Maybe she's tired?

"The weather will change in the next few weeks and that means the migration of snowbirds is upon us." Her ensuing laugh was not as warm as usual.

Maybe she's ready to be away from people in general? What's not to like about downtime?

"Fingers crossed you get to have fun." Tim stood to leave, pointing at his phone. "I'm on the clock, and you probably need to pack."

He walked to the door with Willa trailing him. Just as he reached for the doorknob, he felt the heat of her hand on his arm, scorching a hole through his sleeve. Struggling to ignore the instantaneous lightning bolt to his libido, Tim took a deep breath before turning.

Unfortunately, nothing could prepare him for the punch in the stomach he got from the sight of a sheen of tears covering her eyes. Without another thought, Tim pulled Willa to him, capturing her lips in a molten kiss. Willa didn't push away from him until their connection had reached a heated crescendo equivalent to dancing flames.

When Tim opened his eyes, he found her fingers covering her mouth as silent tears trickled down her cheeks.

"Oh, Willa. I'm so sorry. I didn't mean—"

She held her hand in front of him. "We shouldn't be doing this. Not today."

Hot circles of embarrassment flushed his cheeks, as Tim realized that he'd kissed her without her permission, implying that he didn't need her consent. "Can we talk about it?"

"I can't right now 'cause I'm late getting ready to go." Willa surprised him by reaching out to trace his lips, her fingers shaking slightly against his skin. "But I promise that I'll think about it over the weekend. Right now, you need to leave."

He held his tongue when she reached for the door. When he looked in her eyes, she gave her head an almost imperceptible shake. "It's not you Tim. Please just go."

The single slice of pizza he had eaten sat heavily in his stomach as he returned to his office in the hot sun with his hands buried in his pockets and his shoulders slumped. Not since junior high school had he kissed someone without their permission. Willa's rejection catapulted him back to the afternoon his mother had lectured him about respecting women. Promising her that he would, Tim had never slid backward.

Until today, the best he could hope for was that Willa would return refreshed from her weekend getaway and, at the very least, still want to be friends.

EXTENSIVE RESEARCH CONDUCTED by his team had narrowed the list of participants in the pleasure craft community within Port Lucia to one. With a fleet of catamarans, pontoon boats, and sail boats, Islands & More Water Adventures really was the only operation that had the financial wherewithal to run boats back and forth to the Caribbean and still have plenty for bona fide rentals to cover their facade.

When he brought the company to the commissioner's attention, the man insisted that Tim get a warrant and six investigators to the docks within the hour.

Tim decided their best approach was the front door since it gave them the opportunity to comply with the knock-and-announce rule. When Investigator Darrel Wright had been there two days before, he noticed a flow of people between the front office and the warehouse. Since there was no obvious security locking the door, moving quickly to the warehouse would be easy.

A six-person sweep team of investigators arrived at the main parking lot of Port Lucia at midday. Parking out of sight of their target, two of them would stand watch outside of the offices, just to ensure there were no interruptions. The remainder would execute the search warrant and review records. Sweeps were always a risk for the team. While they had the legal authority to drop in and investigate, many businesses on the wharfs were staffed with concealed-carry staff.

"I'm Special Investigator Monica Dearborn with the Banyan Tree Bay Police Department." Tim watched the coloring on the woman behind the counter blanche when the lead investigator introduced herself. "Are you the owner?"

The frightened woman shook her head and leaned forward while reaching down, causing the four officers to draw their guns while Special Investigator Dearborn yelled for her to show her hands.

"So sorry," her words carried a Latin lilt. "Just pressing the button for the boss to come up front from the warehouse."

No sooner was she finished with the sentence when two from the BTB team charged past the woman, across the office, and through a back door with their guns still drawn.

"Ma'am, please stand by that wall with your hands over your head."

Tim was relieved to hear Dearborn order her away from the counter, lessening the chance for her to grab a weapon. Moments later, Officers Wright and Ortiz led a deeply tan Caucasian in his late forties into the office.

"What is going on in here?" His angry question filled the already crowded space as he yanked his arms away from the officers. "I know the chief of police and I will have every one of your badges. Before you know it, you will be living under a bridge."

Ignoring the threat, Tim started to chuckle as he stepped forward, badge in one hand, drawn gun still in the other. "Allow me to introduce myself," he moved the badge to within three inches of the man's face. "Tim Harley, Chief of Police." He paused a second, his eyes never leaving the man's face. "I don't believe we've ever had the pleasure of meeting, Mister..." Tim slipped the badge into his shirt pocket and extended his hand to the man.

"Lyons. Michael Lyons."

"Are you the owner?"

After a furtive glance around at the guns still drawn, he nodded his head.

"Is that a yes?" Tim had lowered his own weapon but still held it by his side. "Mr. Lyons?"

"Yes. Yes."

Tim felt the angry spittle that accompanied his words.

"Now what do you want?"

Tim holstered his weapon and withdrew the search warrant from his left back pocket. "We have a fully executed search warrant for these premises, including files, vessels, and the building. None of your employees are to leave, you will make them available for a private interview with no coercion on your part. Do I make myself clear?"

"Yes."

Tim noticed a slight tremor in the man's hand when he held the paperwork out to the closest officer, Monica Dearborn. *Hhm, nervous or some form of neurological damage?* He filed it away mentally, intending to reread the files on Michael Lyons when he returned to the office. "Each of you," Tim waved his hand to the owner and receptionist, "are to move a chair to the wall and sit down. Do not attempt to remove anything from your pockets or a desk, or one of these officers will handcuff you."

"Officers Wright and Ortiz, take the warehouse.

Dearborn and Rowling, start in this office. I'll move between both locations." He gave the officers a slight nod of his head, indicating that they were free to re-holster their pieces.

Dearborn and Rowling began pulling ledgers from filing cabinets and storage lockers. As the stack grew higher, Dearborn let out a low whistle and threw a glance Tim's way, communicating without words. He pulled a phone from his pocket and moved through the front door to call for additional officers.

When he came back in, he realized the two officers were methodical in reviewing the heavy, older ledgers. The oversized books reminded Tim of the deed and title records at the county clerk's office in his hometown. The covers were made of thick cardboard wrapped in heavy cotton material in multiple colors—green, blue, and red, all faded from exposure to light.

He kept an eye on the review process of the two officers for a few minutes, taking note of when either one would stop to read a full record rather than just breeze over the names and dates. He couldn't decide what detail caught their collective eyes, but he didn't want to risk interrupting their pattern with questions. Both were exceptional investigators, and the best thing good management could do some days was to just get out of the way.

With the office search well underway, Tim moved to the warehouse, noting that Officers Infante and Ballios had relocated from the entrance of the business to the giant overhead door of the warehouse. At that vantage point, they were able to cover all three openings, front, warehouse, and dockside. He remembered days when his captain wouldn't call for backup, leaving him and his partner to cover too much space and too many doors. Knowing that was how cops got injured, or killed, Tim was sure they would be grateful when the backup arrived.

Leaving Dearborn and Rowling with volumes of paperwork to look through, he decided to observe Officers Wright and Ortiz. When looking through closed cases, Tim discovered that these two men worked together most of the time. Even though he himself had moved up into the nosebleed section of the department, he hadn't forgotten the unspoken trust that exists between partners. And, trust was a critical factor to protect the lives of the people in blue.

Darrel Wright slid open drawer after drawer on the wall-mounted mechanic's tool storage units. Moving methodically, he ran his fingertips over the various wrenches and sockets. Finding nothing permanently attached or hiding under them, he closed each drawer and moved on to a stash of screwdrivers. He pulled them all out, dropping them into a bucket at his feet. Once he had determined there was nothing hidden under the thin rubber mats, he returned the screwdrivers to their original location.

In the meantime, Wright's partner, Che Ortiz, was busy checking all stalls, garbage containers, and clothing storage in the employee locker rooms. Based upon the scowl on the man's face when he returned to Wright, Tim wondered if Ortiz had come across some unsavory content.

"What's wrong?" With his curiosity peaked, Tim couldn't resist asking the question.

"Aw, nothing chief. But ya know, some people are just pigs." Che held his hands up, "but please don't ask me to describe anything."

Tim tried to not smile at the look on Ortiz's face and let it drop. "You got it." With a nod of his head, he turned to leave the men alone.

Tim returned to the business' office to see how the paperwork review was going. Just as he stepped into the nearly silent office, a tapping sound drew his attention to a large metal desk. A few seconds later, Rowling smiled when he lifted out a false bottom. Within moments, Tim stood over his shoulder as he exposed several more notebooks—smaller, and spiral bound ones. A quick glance at the twisting face of the owner assured Tim they had hit a gold mine of information.

Resisting the urge to rub his hands with glee, he held them out for Derek to hand him the ledgers. "I'll start on these." Tim turned to look through an open door. "Oh, what a comfy looking office."

Moving to the obvious inner lair of Michael Lyons, Tim waited until he was in the doorway to glance back at the man. "Nice place. Especially on the docks." He smiled at Lyons and walked away. With an office so plush and palatial, just sitting in the chair was tantamount to hitting on the man's wife, and Tim knew it.

It took him about twenty minutes to peruse the handwritten notes in the first three journals. Halfway through the fourth and final notebook, the records in front of him were more contemporaneous than the first three had contained. Running his finger down a column of numbers, Tim came to the current week's date. His eyes flashed over the names of various catamarans when a unique one stood out, if only because it was in French: *Pas des Bananes. That's curious.* But his breath stopped when he read through the details of what was labeled as a private charter.

Second Name: *No Bananas*
Captain: Damian Buck
First Mate: None
Destination: USVI, BVI
Leave time: 2 p.m.
Number of guests: 1

Glancing at his phone, Tim realized they had little time left before *No Bananas*' scheduled departure. Leaving the book open on the glass-topped desk, he got up quickly. Stepping through the front office, he turned to Dearborn and Rowling, "No one is to touch anything in there."

Trotting through the warehouse to the dock, his eyes quickly scanned the stern of each boat until he found the *Pas des Bananes*, with the English translation *No Bananas* written in small letters beneath. Disregarding the posted rule of no shoes on the boat, Tim made short work of running down the companionway stairs, pulling the hatch to the starboard engine, and adhering a minute tracking device to the solid side of the opening. Returning to the salon, he nestled a bug above the portside cabinet closest to the door of the cockpit.

Was it coincidence that his perpetually moving friend, with no formal home or specific means of employment, was somehow involved with drug smuggling? Unfortunately for Damian, there were rarely any coincidences in crime. And then, there was the matter of Willa being gone for the weekend. When he felt a small twinge of jealousy, Tim knew in his gut that she would accompany Damian on his trip.

At a slight jog, he returned to the dock doorway, directing his statement to Officer Infante. "Only one boat leaves this dock until I give you the all clear." Pointing to the left he said, "The *No Bananas*. And it should have two travelers, a taller blonde man and an attractive Asian woman. Call for me immediately if there are more than that."

Tim raced into the front office, repeating the order to Dearborn and Rowling. Then he stepped in front of the owner. Staring down at Michael Lyons, he gave him instructions. "Mr. Lyons, in a very short time, you have one more charter leaving. I am willing to spare you the embarrassment of having your clients see your office being raided."

The man's eyes flashed with rage, but he stayed silent.

"You may greet them out front and then use the exterior planking that leads to the docks. I will be watching you from an undisclosed location, so don't make any attempt to run or compromise this investigation."

Tim crossed to the front door. "If you agree to this, get out there, now." He struggled to hold the volume of his voice to a respectable tone.

As he watched the man's back, Tim took a psychological punch in the stomach when he was able to make out the familiar shapes of Willa and Damian coming across the paved lot. Having spent the past two hours feeling like the highest level of heel and nursing his injured pride in silence, the sight of her laughing with Damian—tucked into his side with his arm draped around her body—nearly dropped him right there in the marina office.

Closing his eyes for a second while he took in a deep breath, Tim turned to his second in command. "Dearborn, take over here while I go to a better vantage point."

With a mad dash across the warehouse and down the dock, Tim boarded a cat two slips away, but also owned by Islands & More Water Adventures. On his first trip out to the dock earlier in the afternoon, he noticed this particular vessel because the dark glass surrounding the salon and galley gave a person a great hiding spot. The irony of it being necessary to spy on two people he knew, one of which he was beginning to care for, was not lost on him. "Welcome to southern-style law enforcement, Harley," he mumbled to himself as he pulled the dark slider closed on the slightly rocking boat.

Tim took a deep breath as he monitored Damian moving the fifty-foot cat out of the slip and into the channel that would lead them to the ocean, hoping that neither of his friends were part of an international drug smuggling ring. Even if the BTBPD or the Coast Guard didn't charge and arrest them, they were always in danger from the wrath of an agitated kingpin or overlord. *Please Lord, don't let anything happen to her. Please, please, let it just be a vacation.*

Chapter Eleven

Willa's stomach clenched as an unfamiliar man greeted them at the dock. After engulfing Damian into a giant bear hug, the stranger led them along the floating aluminum surface. The interaction was one of familiarity, leading her to think there was more going on than she knew about. When the other man, whom Damian had introduced to her as Mike, turned to ask her simple inane questions, Willa was surprised to see Damian board the next boat on the pier. *How does he know which one we're taking?*

"Hey dollface, throw me your bag," he shouted over Mike's head.

Without breaking the interaction, Willa sidled close enough to the white craft to give her knapsack a hefty toss, hitting him in the chest.

"Jesus, what do you have in here? Bricks?"

"Pipe down." Mike laughed at Damian and turned to

her. "Have a lovely weekend on the water. Your boyfriend is an excellent captain, so you're in good hands." Giving her a tip of his head, the man fled back to the large building he had come out of, causing the dock to bounce under his weight.

"Come on." Damian stood on the side rail of the already idling boat, offering his hand to Willa.

After removing her sandals, she scampered up the plastic block of stairs while balancing herself with the anchor of his hand.

With both feet firmly on the starboard walkway, she looked up at Damian. "Do you know him?" For a second, she thought he would look away to avoid her studying his eyes, but he didn't.

"Who, Mike?" He waved in the direction of the building, "Yeah, we met one night in the Parrot. I think it was right around the time he opened this place. He's a good egg."

"So, you've used his boats before?" She stood firmly, one hand on her hip.

"On occasion."

"How many women have you taken for a romantic weekend at sea?"

That was the question he avoided, looking over her head instead of at her face. "None. Absolutely none. Now, can we get out of here? I want to be through the Keys before dark."

Without waiting for her answer, he grasped her

shoulders and spun her around, giving her a swat on her rump. This intimate interaction surprised her because this was new to their relationship. Once again, her stomach knotted with unexplained ambivalence.

Willa ran her finger along the polished fiberglass surface of the shell of the *No Bananas* while moving around the catamaran. She found it interesting that the name on the stern was actually printed in French with an English subtitle. As no stranger to boating, Willa couldn't remember the last time she'd seen that method of labeling. Another question she would need to direct to Damian at some point. If he didn't know already, by Monday he would realize how much of an organizational freak she was. In her head, things needed to make sense before she was comfortable accepting them.

Willa looked up when she realized that the *pat-patting* of his bare feet had stopped and she found him staring at her.

"Captain's quarters are on this side," he pointed down a small set of stairs. "The other side is for guests. But since we won't have anyone traveling with us, the lights and air conditioning are off on that side."

She nodded at him, hoping the questions in her head would remain silent instead of flying from her lips. She really did want this weekend to be low key and enjoyable. Asking too many things may very well set him on the defensive and put him in a bad mood.

"Is it alright if I go down to unpack?" From past experience, she knew that different captains had different rules about passengers once they'd left the slip.

"I'm going to put your bag down here first. If you can wait until we reach the canal to unpack, I'd like that." He pointed to the banquette in the salon. "Grab a beverage there and have a seat. Or you can join me in the control room."

She opened the small fridge to inventory the contents. Early that morning, Damian had told her there was no need for her to think about bringing anything to eat or drink; he'd mentioned the boat would be fully stocked with food and beverages. As she chose a bottle of water, she caught sight of a few types of cheese, sliced luncheon meat, and butter. She would figure out whatever was beneath those items later. Surely her belly would stop clenching as she relaxed on the open water.

Willa gazed around the salon. In the forward bulkhead, she saw a small library of books shelved on the window ledge, over the big cushions of the banquette seating, along with many house plants. She couldn't remember the last time she'd seen a salon with so many. To the right side, two huge baskets held fresh fruit and bread products, along with several boxes and bags of dried snacks. She noticed potato chips, wheat crackers, a tin of mixed nuts, and a huge bag of candy bars. *Who did they pack all that for?* Reminding herself that she and Damian rarely spent time "hanging out," she really didn't know if he even liked sweets. Beer and alcohol? Yes, resoundingly. But chocolate?

Coming up the stairs, Damian wore a sheepish smile. “What do ya think?” He waved his arms around the space. “Can you handle it for a few days?”

When she looked into his eyes, Willa saw insecurity. “It’s great. Nice place with beautiful wood trim.”

Pulling her to him, Damian placed a tender kiss on her lips. “Good. I like that. Are you joining me topside?”

“Yes. Lead the way.” She gave him a wide smile—hoping he wouldn’t see the questions in her eyes—and held out her hand. Damian lifted it and kissed her knuckles before stepping through the sliding glass door separating the salon from the cockpit lounge.

SEVERAL HOURS after leaving the warehouse and office of Islands & More, Tim sat in his room at the Pink Flamingo. With the white noise of the tv keeping him company while he devoured a fresh mixed meat Italian sub, he planned his weekend in his head. Since the next two days were expected to be full-on hopping days in Banyan Tree Bay, he decided to move into the new place on Monday, if Vera approved.

As he assessed the boxes and suitcases containing his personal belongings, he knew he would also need to do a major shopping trip. Even though Willa had furnished it, he had no idea whether she included dishes, cleaning supplies, or paper products. His cheeks filled with heat remembering how excited he was when she'd offered the place to him. But in his haste to come to a decision, he hadn't bothered to look in the kitchen or bathroom cabinets to see if there was anything for him to use for the first few days. And with the drug investigation hanging over his head, he wasn't sure when he'd get another chance to return to handling daily—or weekly—routine functions like going shopping.

"Ha! Ever thought of the whole online thingy?" Shaking his head, he saw a weather alert pop up on the television screen. Wiping his hands of the mess of oil and vinegar coating them in a slick sheen first, he picked up the remote to increase the volume of the familiar blonde meteorologist. Even when she delivered bad news, he thought she was beautiful. Tim laughed at himself for the secret crush he'd had on Bailey Wilkins ever since she'd worked in Albany.

"Heading into the three-day weekend, those with Eastern Seaboard holiday plans should know that a tropical disturbance in the Atlantic is upgraded to a tropical storm. Gina started spinning in earnest off the shores of Senegal, in the Central Atlantic, threatening the southern half of Florida, including the Keys, and much of the Caribbean with bad weather. At the rate it is moving across open water, Gina is expected to make landfall on Monserrat early Sunday and work her way up the Lesser Antilles to Florida. This storm is very far out, and we'll be keeping track of it."

Tim's jaw hung open staring at the screen. "Willa," her name echoed on his worried voice as it filled the room. "That idiot took her into the path of a possible storm." His stomach clenched as he envisioned her tossed around on the catamaran in the rough seas.

His first thought was to text her about the storm. As he started to type out the words, he remembered that she had asked him to wait for her return to discuss their kiss. If he contacted her now, would she think he was rushing her? He deleted the few words he'd written and put his phone down.

Tim made short work of wrapping up the remainder of his dinner and stuffing it into the tiny refrigerator. Grabbing his keys and the open bottle of water he'd been nursing, Tim jogged from his suite, clicking the door locks on his Jeep in mid-step. He wasn't sure what it would accomplish to be at the emergency command center next to the police station, but at least there would be much larger monitors to see the storm.

WATCHING DAMIAN CONTROL the fifty-foot craft out of its home on the dock and along the canal, Willa was pleased that she'd chosen to be topside. From his standing position at the steering wheel, he nodded to someone on the dock to lift the last tie-off, casting the rope into the stern of the vessel. His eyes roamed the bank of gauges as his gentle touch brought the throttle to life, giving the cat a sense of floating on the water.

A few yards from their slip, Willa noticed someone waving toward the *No Bananas*, and Damian nodding back. The closer they came to the open water, the more she lost track of the number of people who acknowledged them. She wanted to believe it was just the usual friendliness of those who lived on the water, but a few times she'd actually heard Damian's name shouted in greeting.

Not wanting to cloud her brain with her own thoughts of conspiracy, Willa decided to enjoy the much-needed breeze on her skin. When they reached the open water, the deep orange light of the late afternoon sun filled the western sky, teasing of the beauty to come. Willa loved both sunrises and sunsets and looked forward to the next few days when there would be no buildings blocking her sight.

Willa closed her eyes, enjoying the freedom that crept into her soul as the memory of the colorful skyline filled her heart. As a young girl in Thailand, she had spent as many hours as possible on the water with her father, John Davidson. But her mom, Lilly, had reined her in frequently, insisting that Willa learn about the classier side of life. Between etiquette classes, piano and art lessons, and the countless hours her tutor spent on the various languages of the Islands, time spent on her father's sailboat was like being sprung from prison.

"What's the smile for?" Damian's voice interrupted her trip through childhood memories.

"Nothing really. Just enjoying the salt air on my skin." She'd ducked the question with an answer that seemed to satisfy him. Because they had spent much of their time in bars or her bed, they hadn't shared their childhoods. Willa never told him she'd been born in Thailand.

The next two hours flew by quickly with the ocean as smooth as glass. As the early evening surrounded them, Damian navigated to a small bay where buildings and lights speckled the shore. Trolling through the collection of boats bobbing on the water, he pointed to an unoccupied mooring ball and turned to Willa. "Have you ever hooked up to one of those?"

"Yes, a few times, but in daylight." Seconds later a brilliant beam of light fell upon the black surface, the number "32" shining back at her. Something about him flashing the light made Willa bristle. "Oh."

"Yeah, it's a handy tool to have. The hook is on the portside. I'll get a little closer and try to hold steady for you to grab the ball." He looked at her in the fading light. "Don't worry, the water is so calm right now, I don't think you'll have trouble with your balance out there."

"No problem. Give me two minutes to scoot down."

He lifted her off the bench with one hand, kissing her forehead lightly before letting her go. "Thanks, babe. One of the downsides to having privacy is that you become the first mate."

Willa ignored the implication that she had little knowledge of life on a boat. Squeezing his hand in response, she backed down the stairs from the cockpit, picked up the hook, and padded along the portside walkway to the front of the catamaran.

Chapter Twelve

After spending an hour at the emergency center staring at five-foot screens of colored lines going every which way, Tim had a headache. Even though the people in charge of the center were preparing everyone for Gina to hit Florida, there were too many possibilities in the open water of the Atlantic that could change the storm's path.

Tim felt helpless, and in the way, because he could be of no assistance. Moving to his office in the building next door, he took note of the surprised looks on the faces of the second shift as he walked past the squad room. In truth, he had no experience with tropical storms or hurricanes. When Irene hit New York, he was at the point in his career where he took orders from others. But now he faced the challenge of mapping out a plan to prepare the citizens, and visitors, of Banyan Tree Bay to survive the possibility of severe weather.

Staring at the blank lined paper sitting in front of

him, he decided to jot down thoughts: potable water, food for thousands, command center, temporary housing, emergency vehicles. With his hand poised above the pad, Willa's face popped into his mind. *Where is she? Does she know about the storm? What was Damian thinking?* Tim knew she could swim, but doubted she had any experience in the churning waters of an angry ocean.

Twenty minutes and a fresh cup of coffee later, he had created a huge necessities list, worked out the priorities on steps, and written an outline. Even though he had no intention of sharing this info with anyone, he felt better for preparing—if only in his head.

Not giving himself a chance to overanalyze his notes, Tim opened his email and started with step one—a short email to Commissioner Rivers. Due to the swiftly moving storm, he suggested a meeting between the top brass of BTBPD, the emergency center, and the mayor's office as soon as possible. He also recommended rescinding any immediately scheduled vacation time approved to staff members across those three entities. *Way to go, Harley. Aren't you going to be popular!*

Sorting through the pile of longhand notes he'd created, Tim was surprised when the annoying 'ding' of an incoming email interrupted his thoughts. He opened the missive after staring at the red exclamation point for a moment. The sight of it always had an effect on him—usually a negative one. With his breathing noticeably increased, Tim opened the email to find a single line:

Be in my office at 9AM.

Surprisingly, the command from his boss had a soothing effect on him. Feeling as if he'd accomplished at least one thing during his panic, Tim finished sorting through his notes, locked up his office, and returned to the Pink Flamingo. After brushing his teeth and stripping off his clothes, he flopped into bed, rapidly dropping into a deep sleep with vignettes of time spent with Willa putting a smile on his face.

WAKING up on their first morning at sea, Willa quietly climbed from the primary bed, wearing her usual lightweight shorts and a tank, and gently closed the door behind her. When she heard the tiny *snick* of the hardware, she turned in the companionway and tip-toed up to the galley.

Since Damian frequently slept until mid-morning, she had prepped the coffee pot just for herself the night before. As the silken black magic filled her cup, Willa noticed the wind coming from the east was a bit blustery. As the boat rocked in the deepening troughs, she pulled on the sweatshirt she had left on the banquette seat the night before.

Willa cradled a mug of morning joy, happy to also

have the snuggly warmth of her favorite hoodie. Opening the large glass panel, she stepped out to the cockpit lounge and drew a deep breath. Wrapped in the early promise of a new day, she padded to the stern deck and stared across open water, thankful they had taken an outer row mooring buoy when they arrived.

Willa made a quick trip around the deck, being careful not to trip on anything in the pre-dawn light. When they had left Port Lucia, she was very happy to see that the *No Bananas* was tidy, and well organized with secure hanging locations for all of the aluminum tools they used to maneuver the vessel. She even noticed that Damian had hung up the rod she'd used to snag the ball the night before. *Hhm, maybe that Mike guy was right and Damian is a good captain.*

Willa returned to the galley to refresh her coffee, then sat under the hardtop covering the cockpit lounge. With the open lines of the spacious craft, she was able to rest her mug under cover, but still see the slowly rising sun directly to the east. Slipping her phone from the pocket of her sweatshirt, she began snapping pictures as the red orb broke over the point where the water met the sky. The old seafaring adage: *Red sky at night, sailor's delight. Red sky at morning, sailors take warning* popped into her head. She tamped down the nervousness she felt.

She stepped out from under the hardtop to look at the other boats in the cove when she heard the motors of a few other vessels come to life. Much to her surprise, she discovered that the low light of the early morning sky hid many empty mooring balls. Shaking her head in confusion, she knew they had trolled through here last night before choosing their tie-off spot at the opening of the bay, and all of these had been occupied. Why would that many boats venture out so early?

Returning to the covered lounge, Willa watched as the crew on the catamarans to either side of *No Bananas* untethered their vessels. On a gust of wind, the cat rocked deeply, causing her to hold on to a railing to keep her balance. On their starboard side, another catamaran inched away from where she stood, their captain being very polite by not creating any additional disturbing waves in their wake.

"Hello on board from your portside."

Willa spun to the door, expecting Damian to be standing there.

"Good morning, ma'am." She turned to her left to find a lithe man with salt and pepper hair on the neighboring cat. "Just wanted to say that you're the last one in the bay now. Be mindful—there is a big storm coming in."

Willa waved to him. "Thank you. Any idea when it's expected?"

"Sorry ma'am, but the weather folks are still watching that. But last night they upgraded it from a disturbance to a depression. And then this morning to a tropical storm, they've even named it now. She's Gina." Willa smiled at the chuckle that accompanied his last sentence. Many sailors thought it funny to liken the rage of a storm to that of a woman. “I don’t usually interfere with other folks and how they handle their vessel, but you might want to get out of her path now or move in much closer to land. But be mindful that ball won’t be much of a tether in a storm.”

“Thank you. I’ll wake the captain now so we can get moving. Safe travels.”

“You as well milady.” He tipped his head at her and scrambled up to his own flybridge and began the slow trawl away from her.

Willa felt a stone drop in her belly, as if she were being abandoned when a beautiful woman waved goodbye from inside the galley as the craft crept further in the distance.

As the last of their company shrunk on the horizon where the deep red sky met turbulent water, she allowed herself to think about the danger she and Damian were in. Wasting no more time, she trotted to the primary cabin to wake him, crawling across the bed to his side.

“Damian.” She shook his shoulder. “Damian.”

Willa scooted back quickly as his arm swung out at her.

“Leave me alone.” He pulled the covers up over his head.

“Damian, there’s a storm. We need to move. Now.”

“Jaysus, Willa. Go back to sleep will ya. It’s just a thunderstorm.”

“No!” She felt the single word power across her lips

as she grabbed as much of the bedding as she could. “It’s a real storm now. It has a name.”

With a speed and grace she’d never seen from him, Damian bolted from the bed, grabbed his shorts, and dashed to the deck with her right on his heels. First, he squinted at the sky to the east, then did a sweep of the empty bay. “Where’d they all go?” Damian turned on her, grabbing Willa by her upper arms. “When did they all pull out?”

“I don’t know. But the captain of the last one told me about the weather changes. I think we need to move in closer to shore.”

“Yeah, well, I don’t. We need to get moving and get south of this bitch before we get caught in it.” He started toward the flybridge before yelling back at her. “Unhook us from the mooring buoy while I start the engines. Now!”

“Damian,” she yelled as he climbed to the flybridge, “take me home.”

“Are you stupid?” He was hanging from the handrail mounted on the doorway. “It’s too late for that. Go untie us!”

His barked orders reached Willa on the increasing wind, sending a shot of fear to her soul. She hoped to any god that might be watching over her that they would survive this insanity.

THE NEXT MORNING, Tim was practically jogging the few blocks to the station when he thought he heard someone call his name. The second time, he stopped and looked around, finding Willa's friend Jenn waving to him from across the Promenade. Seconds later she was by his side.

"You must really like your new job if you walk this fast to get there." She pointed to the station three blocks away.

"Hi Jenn. Got an important planning meeting this morning with the commissioner. Don't want to be late."

He felt her hand touch his arm before she spoke. "About the storm?"

"What are you talking about?" Tim's eyes scanned the cerulean blue sky totally devoid of clouds. "The weather's beautiful for the first day of a holiday weekend."

"Ha." She dropped her hand and took a step backward. "You can't fool me. I'm an RN, remember? I work at the hospital as the nurse manager of the ER, our emergency plan got dropped into place at midnight. And I know that because my phone keeps dinging and pinging."

Jenn started walking toward the station. "If that

bugger comes too close, I'll be at the hospital 24/7 and I promised Willa I would tend to her store all weekend. I just hope I can get her on the phone."

At the sound of Willa's name, Tim stopped in his tracks. "Do you know where she is?" The log entry in the books at Islands & More Water Adventures flashed before his eyes.

"Not really—just that she and Damian were taking a romantic cruise somewhere. Hopefully they went north in the Gulf where they can dock somewhere safe."

"What aren't you telling me?"

"Oh, it's nothing, just a tiff we had before she left."

Tim kept quiet as Jenn looked toward the ocean.

"She was mad at me because I told her he was a loser. I've never figured out why she thinks he's Mr. Wonderful. There are much better men she could be in a relationship with. Ya know what I mean?"

Pulling a business card from his wallet as she talked, his pulse raced when he saw Jenn tilt her head in his direction. He knew how attractive Willa was, but there was no way he would admit that to her friend before having the opportunity to let Willa know how he felt. "Jenn, I have to run. If you hear from Willa, please call me." He gave her the card and shook her hand. "Thanks."

"Sure thing."

He smiled gently at her and then literally sprinted the last few blocks to his office.

. . .

WITH AN HOUR until he had to be at Commissioner Rivers' office, Tim made a beeline to the desk of Special Investigator Monica Dearborn.

"Morning, chief."

"Good morning, investigator. Grab yourself a cup of coffee and join me in the conference room. I'd like to review where we are on the Islands & More investigation."

"Right away, sir."

While Dearborn collected her file and coffee, Tim made a quick stop in his office. Gazing at the empty desk of his administrative assistant on the way, he wondered if Adrian would be in before Tim had to leave for the meeting.

Rifling through the handwritten notes he'd created the night before, Tim found the one page that was not storm related. After a brief glance at the document, he folded it in half and carried it to meet with Monica. When he reached the conference room on the far side of the squad room, he was surprised to see her already sitting there with her folder open.

"Listen, I have a meeting I have to leave for in a little over forty-five minutes so let's steam roll through some of this." He pointed to the thick file on the table in front of her. Opening his single piece of paper, his hand pressed it to the wooden surface.

"With the perusal you and Rowling did of the more recent ledgers, did you notice any vessels that had been in and out of that marina more than once under the same name?"

"Yes, two."

Tim respected the fact that she stated the information without any emphasis showing on her face or in her voice.

"Names?"

"Vessel one is named *Brittany Boo*, captained by a Leon Graves. Vessel two is *Pas des Bananes/No Bananas*, captained by a Damian Buck."

Tim was prepared for Damian's name to come up, and schooled his face. "Have you created a list of the locations each vessel has been to?"

Dearborn nodded her head.

"And a calculation of the exact number of trips made by each of them weekly, monthly, annually?"

"Yes sir, we have." She paused a moment before continuing. "All locations for both are U.S. Virgin Islands, and the British Virgin Islands." Monica extracted a hard copy of a spreadsheet to show him, pointing to three columns specifically. "Weekly is one each. Monthly is four each. Annually is fifty-two each. Like clockwork, regardless of weather conditions and holidays."

With thoughts of Tropical Storm Gina making her way across the Atlantic, Tim's stomach did a full-blown somersault on him. He pushed his chair back from the table, turning toward Dearborn's questioning face. "Good work. Please tell your team how much I appreciate their effort."

"Thank you, sir. I'll be sure to tell them." Special Investigator Dearborn rose to her full height, leaving her mere inches shorter than Tim's own six feet, four inches.

Tim picked up his single sheet of paper and his coffee again. "I'm hoping to have a new plan for this investigation after the holiday weekend."

As they left the conference room, they acknowledged each other with a single nod and walked in separate directions. Tim already knew he was in for another lengthy meeting with the commissioner after the emergency management meeting ended.

Chapter Thirteen

As the *No Bananas* flew across a huge expanse of open water, Willa realized she had no idea where they were. Ever since they'd left the bay that morning, Damian had been very tight lipped. Any conversation he directed toward her had been unpleasant—as if he blamed her for the change in weather.

Willa had done her best to create cold meals in the galley, knowing it was unsafe to use the gas appliances while the cat was in motion—especially in rough water. Around noon she went to share lunch with him.

"What's that?" His voice was laced with derision as she tried to balance a tray of sandwiches while climbing the starboard side steps.

"I thought you might be hungry."

He dropped his eyes to the food.

"Or at least like some company."

He blatantly snorted at her in response. "What I don't want is you up here whining over the weather."

With their lunch safely balanced on the wide-cushioned bench behind him, Willa turned to leave. "Wait," Damian grabbed her arm firmly. "Take the wheel for a minute. I gotta piss."

Squinting at his use of terminology, Willa grasped the cat's wheel and pushed him away from her.

"Don't be spinning that thing around. Just hold it at top center."

Looking across the waves, Willa thought about their conversations since the day had started. Nothing she had said to him could be construed as bitchy, whiney, or even mean. True, she thought they should have stayed in the bay, protected from the winds by the sloping hills that curved around the water. But now that they appeared to have outwitted the thunderstorm she'd seen on the horizon, she had to agree that Damian had been correct. Even when she complimented him later on the decision, he'd barked at her instead of just accepting her words gracefully. "Ya know, I'm not just some fucking pretty face around here."

When he returned to the flybridge, carrying a half-eaten sandwich, she took a brief look at the tachometer. With his head inclined at her, Damian took back control of the wheel. "I'll do this." He glanced backward at the two sandwiches on the tray. "Might as well take that with you. I don't like that bread, so I made my own."

Willa's anger spiked as he waved the remains of his limp bologna-on-white-bread sandwich. *Why have I never seen this boorish side of him?* Knowing she didn't want to start a fight with him so far away from those she loved and trusted—let alone the fact that her only escape route was to jump overboard—she gave him a wan smile, picked up the tray, and made her way back to the galley.

As she went about cleaning up the mess he had made on the diminutive counters, Willa felt tears of anger working their way out of her eyes. After allowing a few to fall, she wiped her cheeks. "You are not going to cry over someone who is acting like an asshole."

Unexpectedly, Tim's smiling face popped into her mind. It felt good to see the twinkle of his brilliant blue eyes. As her lids fluttered closed, she felt his arm around her shoulders, pulling her tight to his warm chest. She really missed how safe she felt around the chief.

With her resolve strengthened, she stepped out on the stern deck to peek up at Damian, a smile crossing her face when she saw he had both hands firmly gripping the wheel, the muscles in his forearms bulging from the effort.

Finding him fully distracted topside at the controls, Willa ducked back into the salon to look through the multiple cupboards for physical maps, hopefully with delineation lines for American waters. Satisfied with what she found, Willa scooted to the head of the starboard cabin to give herself some privacy.

While she waited for the blue balloon on her phone's map to recognize where they were, Willa opened the map across the sink. When her phone vibrated, after taking a deep breath, she looked down, instantly gasping in shock to see they were in Cuban waters.

TIM WASN'T SURPRISED to hear his name uttered softly as the attendees of the emergency management meeting left the commissioner's conference room. In the few short weeks he'd been working for Theodore Rivers, Tim had found him to be far more than a political hack. This man cared for the officers just as much as the people of Banyan Tree Bay.

"Chief Harley, please stay for a moment."

"Of course, commissioner."

"Call me Theo. Titles are only necessary when there are others in the room with us."

"Thank you, sir. I appreciate that."

When the heavy wooden door closed behind the last staff member from emergency services, Theo spoke again. "I understand you had a busy day at Port Lucia yesterday. I'll assume you have an update for me."

"Yes, I do. Special Investigator Dearborn was quite thorough in analyzing and tabulating the information found in volumes of ledgers from Islands & More Water Adventures. Our suspicion of the company appears to be accurate, specifically for two vessels in their fleet."

Theo nodded for him to continue.

"The two we will be focusing on are: Vessel one, *Brittany Boo*, captained by a Leon Graves. Vessel two, *Pas des Bananes/No Bananas*, captained by a Damian Buck. Dearborn is running background checks now on the two men."

"What has you focusing on those two in particular?"

"Both catamarans have been traveling to the U.S. Virgin Islands and the British Virgin Islands multiple times in the past two years."

Theo raised his eyebrows a second. "But this is southwest Florida. Those could be standard pleasure cruises. You know, college party boats, bridal or groom parties."

"We understand that sir, but the numbers and guest lists are quite questionable. For each cat, the number of trips made from Port Lucia with these specific men at the helm are consistently once a week, four times a month, and fifty-two times a year. They happened like clockwork, regardless of weather conditions and holidays."

"No, that sounds like a very structured tour schedule." Rivers shook his head slowly, obviously not in sync with Tim and the lead investigator.

"Sir, until this week, none of the records show the count of a single first mate or passenger. That's a lot of fuel and wear and tear on the vessels for no one to be paying for the trip."

"And the passenger—is there a way to identify that person?"

"Not definitively yet, sir. But officers at the scene

described her as a tallish Asian woman." Tim knew there would be hell to pay if his friendship with Willa came out before he stepped forward with the info. But at this moment, he was more worried about her safety in the pending storm than his job. What no one in Banyan Tree Bay knew was that Tim had a one-year hold on his job back in Albany. A definite perk of the civil service system in his home state's capitol city.

"Okay. Considering the weather possibilities we face, this investigation can be put on hold until the middle of next week. If things get nasty, we'll need that special team of investigators to help out the uniformed officers."

"Understood, sir." Both men rose from the table. "Theo, I had planned on moving into a new apartment over the weekend. I already gave my notice to the place where I'm staying."

"Oh, yes. The garish pink place that Howard's sister owns." The shorter man chuckled and shook his head.

"With the possibility of Sunday being a wash out, I'd like to take some time off this afternoon to move my belongings and hopefully get a small amount of shopping in. Would that be okay with you?"

"Of course it is." Rivers clapped him on the shoulder as they started to walk out of the wood-paneled room. "You didn't need to ask, anyway. As long as I can reach you on that phone," he pointed to the city issued iPhone on Tim's right hip. "I'm not interested in tracking your every movement. You do get to have a private life here."

Tim laughed in response, not sure that he fully

believed the commissioner. When it came time for him to divulge his relationship with Damian and Willa, he was sure suspicion would surround him until the investigation was over.

When they reached the door to Theo's office, the older man extended his hand. "Have a good day, Tim. Fingers crossed that we don't need to speak before next Tuesday."

Tim tried to hold in the barking laugh that threatened to fill the hallway, suppressing it to a tight-lipped smile instead. "Agreed, sir. Agreed."

When he finally made it to the street in front of city hall, he released a long-held breath. "I need to speak to John." His twin brother had dealt with high-profile cases during his twenty-plus years with the New York State Police. Surely, he would be able to help Tim sort out some of the pieces here.

FOR WHAT WAS EASILY the two-hundredth time, Tim questioned the logic he'd applied when accepting the job. Seriously, who moves to one of the most southern locations in the country during the summer? And what would make a very white and lightly freckled man of Irish descent think his skin would survive the unrelenting sun in Banyan Tree Bay?

"You're a meathead." Admonishing himself yet again as he carried the final box up to his second-floor abode, Tim dropped the forty-pound weight inside the doorway and went to the sink. Even though the commissioner had given him permission to move his belongings into the apartment, Tim had decided not to change into lighterweight clothing before starting the project.

The investigation into Islands & More, including the possibility of Damian and Willa being involved, niggled his brain. If Dearborn called requesting his immediate presence at the station, he wanted to be ready.

Looking down at his sweat-soaked shirt, he had to acknowledge the weakness in his decision-making. After he downed two full glasses of water, Tim peeled off his Ralph Lauren polo on the way to the primary suite. Dropping the phone on the soft green duvet covering an inviting king-sized bed, the rest of his outfit came off faster than his shirt. At that moment, all he could think of was cooling off in the palatial, double-headed shower.

Leaning forward, the ice-cold water splashed over his head, and down his back. He groaned in pleasure at the instant temperature drop of his body, even if the semi-freezing rivulets escaping down his chest, and lower, were causing his manhood to quickly turtle into warmer accommodations. After a few minutes of torture, he spun the stainless handle closer to the red marking.

Filling his left hand with the shampoo Willa had left in the shower, the steamy air turned thick with her scent as the bubbles slid from his shoulders and across his chest, on their way to the drain. He threw his head back in laughter as he felt his penis pushing its way out of hiding. "Oh boy, are you an easy mark."

Tim did a quick cleanup of what he assumed were the smelliest parts of his body. When his bubble-laden hand skimmed up his erection, the teasing smile of Willa popped into his mind. Looking up at the pulsating double heads a moment while continuing to stroke himself, he wondered if she had designed the shower. With one hand pressing against the solid wall of beige onyx, the other hand moved quickly, encouraging his tender manhood to stretch to a painfully new size as a bikini-clad Willa sashayed across his mind, her beauty protected behind his closed lids. When she reached up to press her hands to his pointed nipples and her lips found his, Tim fell over the edge and into oblivion, his deep groan of satisfaction echoing in the steamy room.

Leaving the shower on shaky legs, Tim dropped onto the bed for a few minutes, thinking about his fantasy. Eyes closed to the natural light pouring in through sheer curtains, he tried to remember the last time he'd thought of a woman, other than Nikki. Yeah, his late wife had been stunning. And not that he'd tell anyone, but her talents with his body had been over-the-top incredible. From their first kiss, until this moment, no other woman had occupied the stage in his mind when masturbating. It had always been Nikki.

He took in a breath so deep that his lungs cried out for release. Apparently, his body was ready to move on. Did that mean his heart was also? Pushing the question from his mind, he sat up quickly and began the task of re-dressing.

Once fully covered in his standard chinos and a polo shirt, he grabbed both phones from the wrinkled duvet and moved to the kitchen. Armed with another glass of ice water, he slid into a chair at the small blonde table and opened his personal cell phone.

"Hey, big brother." His voice echoed a little in the generous open space. "Got a few minutes?"

"Sure thing, little brother. What's up? We haven't heard from you in a few days. Does that mean you're settling in with beach life?"

"Yeah, well, I'm about to take out stock in a company that makes sunblock. This white boy is growing freckles in places that don't even see the sun."

His brother's familiar laugh filled the eat-in kitchen. "Have you ever heard of TMI? I don't need to know if you've developed brown spots on your Johnson."

Tim waited for John to stop laughing at himself. "Maybe I have. Or maybe I always had them." His soft monotone set his twin off in another round of raucous laughter.

"Oh, man. Did you call to make me nauseous or to ask me something?"

"I'd like to bounce a case off of you. I know you love what you and Kara are doing with the dogs and horses, but do you think you can put your dusty old cop hat on for this?"

"That I can. What's going on?"

STARING at the phone in disbelief, Willa's body started to shake. "Breathe girl, breathe." she whispered to herself in the small space. That was the moment she realized that the catamaran had stopped its deep rocking. Folding up the unused paper map as quickly as possible, she bolted from the bathroom before Damian could find her with it.

Willa crossed the thick fiberglass floor of the salon silently, opening the cabinet over the captain's desk and sliding the map inside. Only then did she look through the smokey tint of the wrap-around window to see a cutter with the distinct Cuban flag approaching them. Instant fear filled her body, causing her to clamp her hands over her mouth, holding back the scream in her chest at the sight of multiple machine guns pointed at their vessel, she slipped down the stairs to hide.

Chapter Fourteen

As the *No Bananas* came to a complete stop, Willa pulled the sliding glass door to the salon closed, hoping the Cuban officials wouldn't search the catamaran after boarding. Standing on the bottom step of the portside stairs to the primary cabin, her heart hammered in her chest as she tried to listen to the conversation between Damian and the armed men.

"Oh. It's you again, Mr. Buck." The man speaking nodded to the others, causing them to lower their deadly weapons.

How does he know Damian?

"Where are you heading today?"

"Buenos días, general." Damian snorted slightly. "You know me, Charlotte Amalie." She saw Damian lean against the hardtop, his muscles showing no sign of stress.

"Ah, USVI. And back? When should I expect you to arrive?"

The man's thick accent made it hard for Willa to catch everything he said from her hiding spot.

"Tuesday afternoon, maybe Wednesday." Silent sparks exploded in Willa's head at his response. *Tuesday? Wednesday? He has no intention of getting back by Monday? What about my business? And Jenn will be worried about me. And why would the Cubans ask when he would be arriving?* Pushing her anger and confusion to the side, she struggled to hear the rest of their conversation.

"No. No. You know, I always travel alone." Damian moved toward the stern deck where the Cuban authorities had tethered their dinghy to *No Bananas*. "Women on a boat are almost as much trouble as bananas on a boat. Maybe I should change the name?"

The men roared with laughter as they disembarked. But before he began the descent, the man Damian had referred to as general stepped closer to him. "You know the rules. No funny business and we'll all be winners." The Cuban leader offered his hand, giving Damian a powerful shake that caused the muscles on his right side to flex under the lightweight shirt he wore.

Willa wasn't able to breathe freely until she could no longer read the letters on the back of the cutter. Even though she'd lived in another country for many years, never had she experienced the fear of this interaction.

"FILL me in on what you aren't telling me about the case."

Tim wondered whether John would be able to read through his words even though over eighteen hundred miles separated them. "Do you remember my friend from college, Damian?"

"Of course. The spoiled preppy from Long Island. Mom was always afraid he would lead you into trouble. Doesn't he live near Banyan Tree Bay?"

Tim chuckled as he stood to refill his water glass. "Not near, but in."

"Oh, so I assume you've had a chance to catch up over the last few weeks." His brother had a knack for making statements rather than asking questions. Sometimes it felt like he had x-ray vision and could see the words floating around in Tim's mind.

"Yeah. So, the fast forward is this. On the outside, Damian seems like this really chill, surfer dude kind of guy. The people he hangs out with in his favorite bar just love him, especially because he buys lots of drinks. And don't get me started on the employees. He throws so much at them in tips that they think he walks on water."

"Are you jealous, little brother?" John's laugh pealed through the phone.

"Nope, not at all. But my cop mind has been spinning trying to figure him out. He's got no formal residence and no obvious signs of being gainfully employed. Where is the money coming from?"

"I will assume that you already asked him, and he was evasive."

"Yup, absolutely. And got pissed at me when I told him about the new job."

"Didn't he wonder why somebody with your light skin tone wanted to live down there?"

"I think he might have but he keeps his eyes hidden behind sunglasses as much as possible. And he bolted right past his original anger and gave me a line of crap about how he'd throw me a party after I started the new job."

"Tim, how is Damian related to the case?"

"I think he's one of two drug runners working out of a pleasure craft charter business in one of our ports."

"Oh, shit. That's not good. Does the commissioner know you have personal ties to this?"

"No. I decided to see how this weekend played out before telling him."

"What's up with this weekend? You mean 'cause it's a holiday?"

"No, but two other factors. The first one is that as I speak to you, we have a tropical storm barreling at us. Fingers crossed it doesn't turn into a full-blown hurricane. Also, Damian is out with one of the charter boats now and scheduled to be back late Monday. I want to ask him questions first. Also, he has a passenger with him—a woman named Willa."

"How does she play into this? Do you think she's involved?"

Tim shook his head, forgetting that John couldn't see him.

"I've been around her a few times. She's a very bright and driven businesswoman. It seems unlikely she's part of what I suspect Damian of."

"And? What aren't you saying about her?"

"Honestly? She's a really great woman and I'm worried about her being out in the storm. And whatever Damian has gotten her into."

Tim heard his brother suck in his breath.

"Oh boy. I'll assume we're having this little chat because you're uncomfortable with this case. Am I correct? And you need to answer me 'cause this is not a video chat where I can see your face. Next time use one of those, will ya?"

"Yes, I am. I've never had a case where I personally knew a suspect. Let alone being fond of one."

"Of course, you didn't. We Harleys come from much better stock than that. Besides, Mom and Dad would have broken our necks for getting into legal trouble."

Tim lost focus on what his brother was saying when he saw a text from Willa pop up on his phone.

"John, hold on a second, okay?"

"Um, yeah."

Not wanting to lose his chance to connect with her,

Tim tapped out a few feverish responses to her questions. In the end, he felt like he needed to end the call with John in case she called him for something.

"Lay it on me. Do I speak to the commissioner ASAP?"

"Yeah, you do. It's unfortunate you have that storm filling everyone's head with worry, but you need to be up front with this. I've made that mistake before and the clean-up work on my reputation took a while. Trust me on this one." His brother paused a moment. "I suspect this is not the answer you wanted, but it's what I think is best for your career. Not sure about this Willa gal, but you owe Damian no loyalty. However, you do have a big responsibility for Tim Harley, beloved little brother of one of New York's finest. Well, retired finest."

Tim couldn't help but laugh out loud. "Wow. Ego much?" After a few more chuckles to hide his emotion, Tim spoke again. "Thanks, John. I knew you'd be level with me."

"Always, bro. Always. You know where to find me." Seconds later John ended the call, the emotional gravel in his voice wrapping Tim in warm support.

WILLA EMERGED from the salon and climbed to

the flybridge as Damian brought the catamaran up to full speed.

"Who was our company?" She slid onto the bench seat behind him.

"Nobody special." Damian didn't bother to face her.

"They looked pretty official to me—especially all those guns." Willa tried to keep an innocent tone to her voice rather than antagonizing him.

"Jesus, Willa. You don't know what you're talking about. Did you want something?"

He was nicer to the Cubans than he is to me.

She stood up and stepped to the side so she could see his profile. Running her hand up his back, Willa stood on her toes to peck his cheek. "Okay, maybe I don't. But I thought we were gonna have lots of snuggle time, ya know, rocking with the waves." A quick look down at his shorts told her he was listening. "But you've been up here most of the time.

"Later, baby. Right now, I want to get as far as possible before that storm can turn on us." Damian gave her lips a quick brush with his own. "Don't worry, I want to spend time in bed with you, keeping in rhythm with the boat."

She gave his arm a playful swat and returned to the hardtop as a few warm sprinkles of rain peppered her bare skin.

If she wasn't deep in the cat where she had no line of sight of the water, Willa always sat facing backward, eyeballing the horizon. Being a person who preferred the ideology of looking or moving forward in a positive direction, the backward view demoralized her. But staring straight ahead with her eyes focused well above the turbulent water was the only way to keep herself from throwing up. Sea sickness was a pesky problem and she had already taken one antihistamine in an attempt to stop it.

Yuck! Throwing up or curling into a ball on the bed is not an option. With her brain twirling like a whirling dervish, Willa knew she couldn't pass out before answering the questions in her head. Giving up her fight with the rocking boat, she returned to the salon, closing the slider behind her, to sit on the bottom of the companionway steps. The boat's constant motion felt diminished in this position and the sound of the sliding door would alert her of Damian's approach.

Feeling lost and unwanted as a catalyst, Willa sent a text to Tim for the first time since they'd left home.

Hi. You busy?

On the phone with my brother.

Oh, sorry. Never mind.

You ok?

Yeah, sure. Just miss you.

Miss you too. Have fun.

A little demoralized that Tim was busy, Willa

hunkered over her phone, wishing she'd thought to bring her tablet also. For the next hour, she watched the blue pin on the map move out of the Major Antilles and closer to the crystal waters of the Caribbean. Honestly, she didn't know a double hulled vessel could move so quickly.

THE CONVERSATION he'd just had with his brother packed Tim's head as he walked the few short blocks to the police station. When he reached the desk of his assistant, he uttered the words he'd hoped to leave in silence for a few more days.

"Adrian, please see if the commissioner can fit in an immediate meeting with me."

"Yes, chief."

Sitting in the deep, leather chair at his desk, Tim propped his elbows on the glass surface and rested his chin in his steepled hands to wait. *How do I approach him? Start the conversation? What do I say if he fires me? What will happen to Willa in all of this?*

"Chief Harley?"

When Adrian's head poked around the door jamb, Tim realized that the thick, wavey topknot of his hair was a different color than it had been. *How did I not notice that this morning? I think I need some rest.*

"Yes, Adrian."

"He's expecting you in five minutes. Sorry I couldn't get it a bit later but he's running out to the mayor's office soon."

"That's all right. Thanks." Tim rounded the desk, headed to the hallway leading to the street. As he passed Adrian's desk, he pointed to the twenty-something's head. "Nice color change." Before moving completely out of sight, he turned in time to catch the quick smile covering the kid's face.

"HOW IS it you know this man?" The commissioner lowered his face to look over his glasses at Tim.

Part of him wanted to giggle at the comparison his mind was making to his late father, the cop; the parish priest he'd grown up with; and every principal he'd had the pleasure of displeasing, but he knew this wasn't the time.

"We were college roommates."

"When did you last see the man?"

"Probably about ten years ago at our college reunion."

"Did you know he lived in Banyan Tree Bay when you took the job?"

That question threw Tim off a little. "Yes, sir. I did."

"Did you know his form of employment might possibly be illegal?"

"No, sir. I did not."

"Do you believe it is?"

"Honestly, sir—"

The commissioner held up his hand to stop him from speaking.

"I believe I mentioned that you should be comfortable calling me by my first name. Which, by the way, is not 'sir.'" He chuckled softly. "Continue with what you were saying."

"I will admit that the cop side of my brain was already suspicious. But the longtime acquaintance side had always known him to be a perpetual partier, female magnet, money wasting, hail-fellow-well-met kind of guy."

The commissioner let out a single barking laugh. "Ha! That sounded a wee bit like jealousy to me. Did he come from money?"

"Yes, Theo."

"That doesn't mean that he doesn't know how to work. He's just figured out a different manner of applying his knowledge."

"Sir, I'm not splitting hairs here." Tim noticed Rivers' eyebrow arch at him. "Based upon the information that Dearborn and Rowling dug up, he spends more time traveling back and forth to the Virgin Islands than any standard employer/employee relationship would allow time for. Despite knowing him for over twenty years, I find the pattern suspicious."

"Tim, I'm going to give this to you straight. Your past history with the suspect may be a little problematic, depending upon you. Truthfully, you have enough staff so that you don't have to get into the daily ifs and whys of the investigation. But your record of working through those things and proving a good sense for solving cases is part of why we chose you for the job."

Unsure whether the commissioner was done, Tim gave him a slight nod to acknowledge the compliment.

"You have a very good leader in Monica Dearborn. Leave her to manage Rowling and the other men assigned to this case. You should keep a friendly relationship with the suspect until the investigatory process has led you and Monica to a firm conclusion."

Sensing dismissal, Tim rose, scanning the commissioner's face for emotion. Seeing none, he tried to tamp down his nervousness. If this admission cost him his job, he would cross that proverbial bridge when he reached it.

"Thank you for your time, Theo. I know you have a full calendar." Before he reached the door, the commissioner spoke.

"You are the solid cop that Banyan Tree Bay needs as its chief of police. Follow your intuition Tim, and you'll make the correct decisions."

"Thank you." He broke eye contact, pulling the door closed in his wake. When he reached the street, he sent his brother a text.

Thanks for our chat. All is good.

Chapter Fifteen

By morning light, Willa discovered they had anchored about a hundred yards offshore. Damian was not with her, and his side of the bed was cold to the touch. She did her best to tamp down the warning flashes spiking from her head to her belly. *Not another day of stress. I can't do it.* On soft feet, she used the head, brushed her teeth, and splashed water on her face. She considered a quick shower. After yesterday's emotional roller-coaster ride, she wasn't sure when she'd get the chance to take one, but for now, she needed to find Damian.

At the top of the portside companionway, she gazed out at the calm water. *Where are we?* She gave her phone a moment to load a map and for the location pin to pop up. When it did, the tension she'd felt in her neck and shoulders let go. "Thank god, American waters."

"Are you talking to me?"

Willa jumped in surprise at the rough voice, her eyes scanning the salon to find Damian laying on the thick cushions of the banquette seating, a thin fleece blanket pulled up to his neck.

"Sorry, I didn't see you there."

Damian swung his feet to the floor, balancing himself on the edge of the table while he sat up. "No problem. What time is it?"

She tapped on the dark face of her phone. "Early. Just six." Much to her surprise, Damian cast aside the covering, slid over the seat, and stood. After a deep yawn, and a stretch that pulled his shirt up to display his abdomen, he opened his arms to her.

"I'm sorry about yesterday. I don't do well under stress."

She felt his arms wrap firmly around her, instantly causing conflicting feelings to sprout. His delicious body always turned her on, but her head remembered all of the bitter things he'd said to her the day before.

"Now that we've arrived. How about a fresh start on our weekend?"

She raised her gaze to see him give her a sexy and conspiratorial wink. When she saw him incline his head to kiss her, Willa turned her head slightly, directing him to her cheek instead of her lips.

"Don't be mad, baby. I did what I had to for our safety."

Even though she felt standoffish, Willa had no desire

to start another round of fighting. While they were back in U.S. waters, they were still a long way from home. After yesterday's exchange with the Cubans, she had no idea how many people he knew down there, or anything about their loyalty to him. The last thing she wanted was to find herself on the run with no one to trust.

Pushing away from him, she stepped toward the coffee pot, pasting a smile she didn't feel on her face. "How about some coffee to watch the remainder of the sunrise?"

Damian looked out through the cockpit lounge, and then at her. "Sure. I'll put out the cushions." Unlocking the slider, he stepped outside into the clean morning air. Willa watched as he walked to the stern deck, stretched his arms to either side and groaned with pleasure. "Oooo, it's gonna be a beautiful day."

Willa couldn't believe that he'd moved on while she was still jumpy with fear of his behavior. *Let it go. Enjoy the day. You haven't been down here in a few years.* Reaching in the cabinet for the package of dark, loose coffee, Willa drew the scent deep into her lungs, listening to the steel drums in her head as a slight breeze rocked the *No Bananas*.

"Yeah, let's make this a beautiful day," she whispered to herself as she put on the coffee. If she was going to make it through the weekend, she needed to blank out the previous day and a half.

TIM'S PHONE pinged on his walk to the office. At first, he didn't recognize the number, but opened the text anyway.

> Hi. This is Willa's friend Jenn. Just heard from her. They're safe in the Virgin Islands.

Tim shook his head at the amount of water Damian had covered in such a short period of time. Once again, he couldn't decide whether the guy was brash or a hopelessly self-centered jerk. *There was no one else on the boat to help captain. Did he run for twenty-four hours straight?* Not wanting to let Jenn know he had bugged Damian's boat by putting a tracking device on it, which Monica Dearborn was monitoring, he asked her one more question.

> Thanks. Any idea where in VI?

> Yes, Charlotte Amalie.

> Again, thanks.

At least the note from Jenn had relaxed him a little. Willa was safe. In his heart he wanted her to have a good trip. The woman worked very hard and even a few days of downtime should be hers.

Since he was already distracted, Tim decided to pop into a diner for breakfast. Waiting for a server, he reviewed his email, with the first one from the emergency management team. Blinking his eyes, he felt a smile warm his face.

> Gina expected to continue to move straight north, about 200 miles off the coast and then continue further out in the Atlantic. We can expect rain both Saturday and Sunday, but NOAA has dropped the warnings for us.

Tim wanted to shout with joy. One worry was off his plate. At least now Willa and Damian should be able to return safely. His appetite instantly increased with the joy he felt at the unexpected update, so Tim ordered a breakfast better suited for an athlete than a desk-jockey cop in his mid-forties.

WALKING into the quiet police station half an hour later, Tim was glad that he'd worn his favorite pair of deck shoes. His nearly soundless steps carried him to his office without interruption. During night times and weekends, the building was more of an empty shell than the bustling overcrowded police station of a mid-sized city. As a young cop, he didn't really understand why so many of the older guys in his station preferred the quiet shifts. But with that mid-life mindset knocking on his door, he relished a building so quiet that conversation happening in the break room echoed throughout the first floor.

"Chief?"

Tim spun in his chair when he heard Monica Dearborn's voice.

"What are you doing here?"

"Ortiz and Wright were on surveillance last night at Islands & More."

"Oh? I thought we were letting this case sit for the holiday weekend." He motioned for her to take the chair across from his desk.

"Yes, sir. I know what you said. But then my team got into a deep conversation. It turns out that Wright has come across Leon Graves before on cases, when he still worked in Tampa. And, Ortiz remembers the other guy, Buck, from a few skirmishes in his early days in Banyan Tree Bay. Apparently these two are not strangers to law enforcement."

Tim steepled his fingers in front of him while he digested her words. *Damian, you jackass.* "So why the surveillance last night?"

"Two uniforms who cover the bars in Port Lucia heard fresh rumors about a shipment coming in."

"What did they find out?"

"Oddly, when Leon settled into the slip, the only thing he took from the boat with him was a smaller box, maybe eight by eight." Monica held her hands out, shaping imaginary dimensions.

"That size box of drugs wouldn't be worth the cost of going to the Caribbean."

"No, sir. It wouldn't. But precious stones would be."

Tim felt his eyebrows shoot to the top of his forehead. "Well, that would add a whole new set of problems to Mr. Lyons' plate when it comes to the interaction with us. Did Ortiz and Wright...."

A surprisingly loud laugh shot out of the investigators mouth, interrupting his next question. "Ya think? At this rate his business card will read, 'Federal Drug and Jewel Smuggler, Extraordinaire.' And yes, they stayed for several more hours to see if there was any more action on the dock, but nothing."

"I guess if you're in the criminal category, it has a nice ring to it."

As they continued to laugh, Dearborn rose from her chair.

"Don't take any action yet, Dearborn. File the report and video. But do me a favor, make a dupe of both and hand them to me."

"Sure thing, sir. Give me an hour."

"Nice work on the part of Ortiz and Wright."

"Sir, they really are excellent investigators. I'm proud to have them on my team." Monica nodded to Tim and left his office.

Tim's mind did a deep dive about Damian as the officer's footsteps echoed away from him. Even though he'd been skeptical about his friend's means of earning a living, he really hadn't considered that the carefree, surfer-esque party animal he'd known for almost half of his life would be deeply embedded with the ruthless crowd that managed both types of illegal operations.

THE CATAMARAN gently rocked from a ripple of waves caused by vessels in the deeper water. If she let her guard down, Willa knew the movement would tease her into a nap. And she didn't want to waste a single moment in the Caribbean sunshine.

"Do you have plans for the day?" Her voice was nearly a whisper.

"Yes and no. Pretty much depends on you."

She noticed that Damian's eyes never stopped scanning the water when he answered. Her skinned goosied up, realizing she wasn't comfortable with what she saw. *We must be in danger.* When he stood from the bench across the salon table from her, a scowl covered his face.

"Do you want to swim, sunbathe, shop, or," within three steps he wrapped his arms around her, nuzzling the side of her neck, causing new goose bumps even though she had planned on not being turned on by him. "Maybe we can just stay below deck, making this baby rock like that storm came back."

Willa struggled as temptation filled every part of her

body. Yes, he was a talented lover. Yes, she really enjoyed the additional pleasure of making love on a craft small enough to feel the perpetual motion of the water.

Damian took her left hand in his. With a gentle pull, she found herself standing literally toe to toe with him, their bare feet braced against unexpected rocking. His hands slid under her loose tank top and up her ribs, the weight of her untethered breasts filling his hands.

Willa shook her head in disappointment, remembering how Damian had treated her before this morning. With her mind full of conflicting thoughts, she pushed his arms away, leaving her body craving the return of his hands. Without a word, she turned away from him and made her way to the captain's quarters. Once inside, with the door locked, she tossed her tank top on the bed and entered the shower, not waiting for the water to warm up as she would at home.

With her forehead nearly leaning on the back wall, Willa let the water saturate her long hair, on its way to her derriere. Wishing she were anywhere but in the small space, she looked at the ceiling, swearing at her traitorous body. How was she ever to make him see how much his words ripped at her heart when every inch of her had just screamed "do me?"

Kicking her self-pity to the proverbial curb, Willa cleaned her body as quickly as possible, rinsing the conditioner from her hair and then turning off the water. As the last few drops fell from the rainfall shower head, she made a new deal with herself regarding Damian. There would be no more fighting this trip, but also no sex. From this point forward, he would have to believe there was still hope for intimacy because they were too far from home for Willa to piss him off.

Chapter Sixteen

With Dearborn's five-page report seared into his brain, Tim went home to unpack his belongings. He looked forward to no longer living out of a suitcase with high hopes the move would make him feel grounded—like he belonged in the town, even if it was nearly two thousand miles from those he knew and loved.

The sounds of holiday fun came from the backyards of the small neighborhood when he crossed two side streets on his way to Beachside Promenade. People laughing, kids yelling, dogs barking—all accompanied by the redolent scents of food cooking outside. He grinned. *Maybe I can make this place home, in my heart.* If he were being honest with himself, and he tried to be as he'd aged, home was no longer a location on a map. Home was where people supported you and cheered you on, where they checked in on you, where they invited you to join them in various activities. And Banyan Tree

Bay had already given him one special person who did those things for him.

When he reached his front door, Tim looked up at the windows of Willa's place. Unlike when she was around, there were no curtains fluttering against the screen, no music reaching the street, and no laughter. He hoped she was safe in the southern waters. And having fun.

The first thing on his agenda was changing into lighter-weight clothes. With only a few weeks of living in the Bay, he already felt wrapped in an overheated cocoon when he wore what he considered his uniform—khakis, a polo shirt, and loafers. But since it was a weekend, and technically he was off duty since the hurricane decided not to spoil the holiday, shorts and a worn-thin metal band T-shirt were the combination to make him smile.

With classic rock and roll blaring from the stereo Willa had included in the furnishings, he felt good as he looked around at the empty boxes strewn about the apartment. Tim settled himself on the deep sofa, bottle of water in hand, his gaze traveling over the light birch shelves directly below the giant television screen and took a deep breath. Looking at the ridiculous number of framed pictures he had unboxed, his heart swelled, knowing they weren't all from his house in Albany. Many came from his sister-in-law, Kara—the irrepressible redhead who had careened into John's mental space and completed his brother's life. Tim wasn't sure when she'd stashed them in the moving box, but he loved that she included pics of their children, Declan and twins Saoirse and Siobhan, several horse and dog pictures, and one from the day they had dragged him to Lake Placid to hike among the Olympic Mountains.

But the family shots didn't stop there, with several of his other siblings and the many friends that morphed from the John and Kara orbit into his own. Unexpected thoughts about Willa slipped in to shake hands with the ones he'd just had about family. *What would she think of them? Would she like them or find them boorish or less worldly?* Tim shook his head. "Don't stress it, you are a lucky man." He slapped his bare knee and stood up, groaning slightly at the muscles he'd stretched with hours bending over boxes. "Time to go shopping."

WHEN DAMIAN CAME up behind her in the galley, Willa tried not to let his wandering hands have an effect on her. They were magical, she couldn't argue with that. Unfortunately for Damian and their relationship, after they both showered, he took a book up to the flybridge deck while she cooked breakfast. *He should have offered to help*. Or, his time could have been dedicated to setting places to eat, either in the salon or out on the cockpit lounge table, under the hardtop. Instead, he acted like she was his servant.

After cleaning the galley, she'd gone topside to join

him, hoping for light conversation and company. When she slid down onto the spacious sun-bathed cushion, she found him sound asleep, snoring loudly.

Willa moved off the bench and over to the trampoline ropes spanning the distance from one hull to the center of the forward end of the boat. Walking across the woven pattern, she looked at the water surrounding them. Diamonds of sunlight danced on top of the small waves, casting a shimmering pattern across the ocean, accenting the electric shades of the water. With the shore nearly a quarter mile away, everywhere she turned, the colors of turquoise, seafoam green, and white warmed her heart, despite how many times Damian had let her down since they started this trip.

Laying on the sturdy webbing, Willa listened to the rhythmic pattering of the steel drums in her head, accompanied by the gentle melody of the water. The slight *chug-lug* made each time a wave lifted the cat up and down added to the imaginary beating pattern in her mind. As the caressing of the hull's hypnotic rhythm soothed her tired ears, Willa's thoughts slipped to the last conversation she'd had with Jenn.

At the time, she couldn't fully understand what Jenn was saying about how Damian treated her. But with clear eyes, she agreed with her long-time friend. And her assessment of her relationship with Tim.

"Because I've been around you two and I see how you look at each other, the way you coquettishly bump shoulders. I

know there's potential there. The chief's a good man. One who won't hurt you."

The beautifully angled lines of Tim's face popped into her head, his laughter filled her ears, along with the times they had been on the beach together. Each rock of the catamaran increased her desire to drift off into the satisfying dreamland that had become her thoughts of him, the hot cop. In her mind, he was the guy who would treasure her, protect her, and love her. Tim was the guy she deserved, not the jackass who treated her like shit. With the need to sleep intensifying, the gentle rocking of the boat hugged her battered soul, assuring her that nothing more Damian said could hurt her.

TIM LOOPED through the aisles of the monster grocery store he'd found farther out in Banyan Tree Bay. He probably looked silly to other shoppers when he *ooh*ed and *ahh*ed over products he'd never seen in the chains in Upstate New York. With clean, open space, friendly employees, and even friendlier shoppers, he decided that the near-constant sunshine of south Florida was the boon responsible for lifting so many spirits.

Pushing his cart through shimmering heat waves rising from the asphalt and pausing a moment when he heard thunder in the distance, the ten-year-old boy buried deep inside of him wanted to run recklessly to his Jeep, kicking his heels up for fun. Even though he was off the clock, he opted for the chief of police persona instead.

Tim had already learned that thunderstorms in the tropical environment were fast, fierce, and a little bit frightening. Where he had spent most of his life, in the north, there were higher land masses—like mountains and trees, for the lightning to strike. But Banyan Tree Bay was virtually flat, like much of the state. Because of that, cloud-to-ground strikes were common, and storms built up mean-looking balls of black clouds that charged across a space, leaving tree detritus and gleaming sunshine in its wake.

The wind picked up, foretelling the storm to come. In minutes he had stashed the whipping plastic bags in his back seat and returned his cart to the corral. Just as he was about to jog back to his vehicle, he saw an older woman struggling with her own groceries. *Remember, Momma always said to be nice whenever you can.*

He approached the tiny woman with his hands folded in front of him. "Hi ma'am. I'm Tim. Would you like me to put those in the car for you?" When she looked up at him, her soft blue eyes were watering from the wind buffeting her face.

"Thank you. Yes. In the trunk, please."

"Sure thing. You stay right there a moment and make sure I'm doing it right."

"You must be married." The white-haired woman gave him a soft laugh. "Or your mother taught you well."

"Ha, even though she's been gone many years, I can still hear my mom in my head." Tim grabbed a few bags with one hand, placing them on top of the plaid blanket spread across the bottom of the trunk. "And I'm a widower, married almost twenty years to my high school sweetheart. So yeah, I've had my training."

Tim placed the last of the bags inside the car and pulled it closed. Lost in thought about his mom and Nikki, he almost jumped when he felt a slight pressure on his lower arm. "I'm sorry about your wife."

"Thank you."

She shook her head at him. "You look very familiar. Have we met?"

This wasn't the first person to say that since he'd moved to Banyan Tree Bay. He took her right hand and gave her a gentle handshake. "I'm Tim Harley, the new chief of police."

The woman's face came to attention, her eyes lighting up while a smile crossed her delicate cheeks. "How nice to meet you, sir. I'm Lorna. Lorna Michaels."

Taking a quick peek at her left hand, Tim responded. "The pleasure is all mine, Mrs. Michaels." A loud clap of thunder caused Lorna to spin, one hand clamping across her mouth, the other patting down the clear bonnet that covered her snow-white hairdo. Tim placed his hand on one of her elbows, gently steering her toward the driver's side. "Let's get you inside before you're soaked."

Lorna scooted to the door he held open, surprising Tim with her quick step. "Do you need help getting these inside your home?"

"No thank you, chief. I can pull right into the carport in front of the garage. My daughter will bring them in from there." She pointed to the darkening sky. "You better hurry now before you get soaked. Thank you for helping me. It was very nice meeting you, chief. And so refreshing to have a young man protecting the citizens around here."

Tim waited a moment while she closed the door, started the ignition, and clicked her seatbelt around her tiny frame. Just as she put the car into reverse, her window slid down. "And please, call me Lorna."

"I sure will, if you'll call me Tim."

"Only in private young man. Your title deserves respect."

Her soft smile made him happy. "You are most welcome, Lorna. Now try to get home before that old boy soaks all of us."

Giving him a tiny wave, Lorna rolled up the window and backed her car out of its spot and drove away. Even with the dark sky surrounding him, Tim's heart was happy from the interaction. "Yup. This is why you do what you do."

DAMIAN'S WEIGHT on the heavy ropes woke Willa from her nap long before his hand touched her.

"Baby, you're really baking out here."

She rolled to her back and sat up, then stood, her feet wide on the unstable surface. "Yeah, probably shouldn't have fallen asleep."

"Are you interested in cooling off in the water?"

Willa's mind was still comforted by thoughts of Tim as she gazed at the cerulean bath below her feet, watching a small school of tiny fish skitter close to the surface. She shook her head to push away the dreams when she heard Damian ask her a question.

"How about snorkeling?"

"Seriously. This rental has gear on it?" She bent her knees a little to accommodate Damian walking off the netting. *He is such a clod, never offering for me to lead the way.*

"Of course. This is no fly-by-night outfit here." Damian braced his hands on his hips and threw his head back in raucous laughter. "It's named *No Bananas*, not *The Minnow*." He bent down, slapping his own knee at the silly reference to the boat from *Gilligan's Island*.

"Why are you just standing there, captain? Get me

some gear!" Her good mood returned quickly with the opportunity to play in the water.

Willa loved snorkeling. It offered a totally new world below the surface of the ocean. A few minutes later, Damian handed her a wetsuit, fins, and a snorkel sealed in plastic. After preparing herself to use someone else's equipment, the sight of factory-wrapped gear boosted her excitement a notch higher.

"This is brand new?" She turned the lavender rubber in her hands.

"Yes." Damian winked at her and turned back into the salon. "I'll be ready in a minute."

Waiting for Damian, Willa sat down to work on donning the wetsuit. It had been several years since she'd worn one; long enough that she'd forgotten how much it felt like a second skin. Slipping her right foot, then her left, through the full-length suit, she stood up and began the slow tug-of-war to bring it up over her thighs, hips, and derriere. Right after she slid her arms through the sleeves and pulled the zipper closed over her breasts, Damian gave an appreciative whistle.

"Hot baby. You are so hot." He gave her buttocks a firm squeeze.

Willa loved wearing one. In addition to protection from the water temperature changing quickly, the suit gave her additional buoyancy in the salt water, and it minimized resistance, so she was able to swim faster and with less effort. But in truth, her favorite part was that she always felt erotic in a wetsuit. The sleek black neoprene accentuated her curves in a very sexy manner, yet she was fully clothed. And water was her fun zone—soft rain on her skin, a steamy shower, swimming naked. Water made her feel sultry and complete.

Ignoring Damian, Willa's thoughts returned to Tim as she lowered herself to the bottom of the portside transom steps to dangle her feet in the warmth of the Caribbean. *Imagine floating in this perfect water with him.* After adjusting the strap of the mask to fit her head, Willa spit into the lens, smearing the fluid around the surface. In her mind, this was the gross step in snorkeling. *Let's face it, spitting anywhere is gross but then putting it on your face?* But in the world of snorkeling, it was standard practice to prevent the clear lens from fogging up. She gave the mask a quick dunk in the water, wet her cheeks and forehead with a small handful, and pressed the rubber to her skin, pulling the strap over her head. Moments later she slid into the ocean.

Slipping her head beneath the surface for the first time, Willa felt the fissures of fresh excitement stringing through her body. When she heard him enter the water, she spun around to see Damian waving for her to join him on the other side of the boat. *Always the bossy one.* With her legs straight, Willa used a few flutter kicks to cover the distance, thankful she had put on longer fins.

As she accepted the hand he extended, Damian led her down to a clump of lichen-covered rocks and waving sea grass. He winked at her through his mask, having no idea she harbored negative thoughts about him.

Trying not to loosen the seal of the mask, Willa suppressed the need to giggle at the antics of various sea creatures. Brightly colored small fish darted around them, stopping to investigate the flora for mere seconds. In a shallow pool near a rock outcropping, three spider crabs scooted sideways then disappeared into a crevice as she and Damian approached.

Willa looked up when the water around them darkened and found a spotted eagle ray gliding above. The huge and powerful fins to either side of the stingray's nearly pure white belly gracefully pumped, showing the topside of the fish, and the signature white spots filling the three- or four-foot dark-skinned expanse. As the beautiful creature seemed to fly through the water, Willa watched it angle down toward the white sand. Separating the fine grasses to hunt for clams, oysters, shrimp and sea urchins, the large animal hid in the sand clouds it created while digging for food.

Spying a small school of juvenile beau gregory, the deep blue top line freckled with royal blue spots that sprinkled down into the eye-catching yellow belly of the fish, Willa looked around for Damian, hoping to show him the spectacular sight. With no outcroppings or large piles of stone and grass to camouflage him, she thought to look up.

When she found his bronzed legs gently treading water near the portside transom steps, Willa shook her head in disgust at Damian's apparent lack of appreciation for the magical world below them. *How does a person who knows how to snorkel go topside in such a short time?*

Rising to the boat, Willa's thoughts wandered to Tim. *I wonder whether he likes snorkeling. I'll have to ask when I get home.*

Chapter Seventeen

Willa learned as a child that you never go under the water alone. Her dad was always strict about snorkeling or diving in pairs—not that they had done much diving. The idea of rising too quickly and giving herself the dreaded bends was a constant fear. So, when Damian suggested she go back down without him, she was shocked.

"Listen, you've still got some daylight left. You go back down, and I'll start prepping."

"For what?" The hair on the back of her neck did an immediate ten-hut on her wet skin.

"Oh, I thought I told you. Once the tourist cats move out, I want to grab an overnight berth at the dock."

She felt like he held something back. But Willa knew they needed fuel, so it made sense to move closer.

"They have some great vendors set up here. Maybe you'd like to do some shopping tomorrow? After we can catch some lunch."

Still not convinced he was giving it to her straight, but insatiably drawn to the water, Willa gave in. "Okay. But I'm going to tie off. Give my line a tug if you need me."

The silver dinghy tied to the *No Bananas* slapped the water as it bounced on the wave of a passing craft, splashing Willa's hands as she tied the stern rope to her waist. Next, she began the process of resealing her mask.

After sliding into the water, Willa pulled on the tether a few times to test the knot. The lightweight rope wouldn't let her go more than three hundred feet from the boat, a comforting thought to Willa since she was going below by herself, and she knew she tended to get distracted easily by the unmatched beauty of the ocean.

Allowing herself to move slowly through the tepid sea, she listened to the under-surface sounds surrounding her. Losing herself to the soft gulps and burps, the ever-moving ocean worked its cathartic magic as she skimmed along gracefully, watching the sea life go about its daily business of surviving.

For Willa, it never got old watching the beams of light dancing across rocks, sand, and reefs, in the azure waters. The Caribbean was such a beautiful environment to submerge oneself in and her thoughts once again turned to Tim, picturing him by her side. With an occasional single flip of her fins, she floated amongst schools of silver fish, including the shimmering bar jack and the rainbow runner. Looking to her other side, she discovered clusters of smaller fish with neon colors of orange, yellow, and green.

Willa chuckled inside her mask when a few blue tang scooted under her torso. Ever since the movie *Finding Nemo* blew into everyone's lives, the mostly deep blue fish, with a small yellow spike where the tail met its body, was instantly recognizable.

As sunlight flashed off nearly albino skin as it alternated with the black striped pattern of the banded butterfly fish, Willa glanced down in the water. Perched on ledges that resembled rocks but were soft, fibrous, living plant life, green and gold leaves waved at her. Their flexible bodies allowed the long, thin, gray abdomens of the flat needlefish to serpentine among them. The hydrocorals in browns, reds, and pinks seemed like conch shells to the inexperienced eye. But the plant she was most drawn to had to be the waving branches of the Christmas tree coral, with its beautiful luminescent branches ending with soft blue, yellow and red flowers.

The brilliant and flowy life of the world beneath the water always delighted Willa. Some days she wished that every person alive could have this ethereal experience. But when she caught sight of a school of lionfish, she recalled an article that said humans were most likely responsible for the spread of the hyper-invasive species of fish that were doing a staggering amount of damage to the reefs in the Western Atlantic. As a little girl in Thailand, the lionfish was a common dish on her family's table. No one liked capturing the spiny creature with its weird, spikey, feather-like quills jutting out from several spots on the body, but the white meat was delicious. Politely watching the fish from a distance, Willa made a mental note to report them to the US Virgin Islands hotline for NOAA.

With her focus on the invasive fish, Willa spun quickly at the slight tugging she felt on her safety rope. Looking up, she saw the *No Bananas* rocking on the surface, indicating an increase in the waves. Seconds later, the muffled sound of a motor reached her ears.

Willa crossed the distance between her and the cat, slicing through the water as quickly as she could, surfacing between the two hulls. Despite the water slapping on the bottom of the vessel, she was careful not to make a sound. With a very light touch, she placed one hand on the fiberglass surface to steady herself while she pulled off her snorkeling mask with the other.

She could hear at least two strange voices talking to Damian, possibly passengers in the unknown dinghy that had pulled up behind the catamaran. There was no mistaking a round of friendly laughter from the visitors and Damian, but what she could distinguish was sporadic, leaving her trying to make sense of the word salad.

"Thanks for the payment."

She heard Damian mutter something in response. A few short moments later she heard the dinghy motor come to life before shooting into her line of sight between the hulls. To Willa, they appeared to be dark-skinned native islanders, both wearing a large, floppy hat which conveniently hid their identity from anyone looking.

WITH A QUICK GLANCE down the alley that served as beach access by his apartment, Tim found chaos on the near perfect white sand. Getting out of his car, he walked about fifty feet closer to the water to see beach goers packing up their belongings in a hurry with the arrival of the storm. Many threw hastily folded blankets into oversized bags or wagons. Several small children screamed in fear, searching for their parents at the crack of thunder. One man successfully grabbed an umbrella just as it started to flip inside out, while another umbrella became an unexpected weapon as it came flying horizontally through the moist and sandy air, propelled by giant gusts of wind.

The umbrella pitched downward, causing it to embed into the soft sand. Safely protected from the mayhem, Tim's mouth rounded in surprise as multiple flying palm fronds dropped onto the now-mangled umbrella, the weight of the giant, wet leaves pinning it to the ground. As if unfazed by the danger, gulls and pelicans continued to fly, even though the wind ripped away their squawking at each other. Another giant gust caught a few of the nuisance birds, tossing them through the air and into the rough surf. Tim was surprised to see the birds surface quickly and launch themselves into the turbulent sky again.

Countless numbers of people raced past him, their arms loaded with belongings and children, on the way to the safety of the overhangs and awnings on Beachside Promenade.

Thoughts of Willa on the catamaran in this wind threatened to tank his mood. *This is just a thunderstorm, but over the water it might be much worse.*

As the sky continued to darken, he made a few quick trips to bring his groceries upstairs. He slipped the easily perishable items in the fridge and then trotted back to his Jeep to move it to a close lot. Opening the driver's side door, Tim burst into uproarious laughter at the sight of a parking ticket tucked under the windshield wiper. "Imagine that, old man—you are an official Banyan Tree Bay scofflaw." Still chuckling, he yanked the heavy-weight paper and tossed it inside the car as he slid into the driver's seat.

NOT WILLING TO RISK TRIGGERING DAMIAN into another outburst, Willa waited a minute before moving to the transom steps to leave the water. Sitting on the textured surface, she pulled off each fin, placing them and the mask on the step behind her. Then she drew in her rope, wrapping it into a large loop and hanging it from the inside of the railing, next to a life vest and preserver. Turning away from the water as she rose to her feet, she saw Damian step out of the salon carrying a bottle of water.

"How was your quest? See any sharks or barracudas?"

"Ha, no! I wouldn't have been out so long if I had." Reaching down for the freshwater hose to rinse off her equipment, she distracted herself for a couple of minutes. "Did I hear company come to call? Anyone special?"

"Oh, yeah. No one special, just looking for rent money on our anchor." He pointed his hand to the forward end of the boat, his eyes not meeting hers.

"But we're not on a mooring ball. Why should we pay anything?"

"I don't know, sweet cheeks. But when two men obviously wearing hardware hold out their hands for money, I give them some." He shook his head as if he thought her question was ridiculous.

Willa stowed her gear in the large hold under the lounge mattress while he watched her from inside the salon. When she stepped through the large sliding glass door, Damian looked up from his cell phone for a second. "Why don't you take a quick shower and I'll put together a snack for us. Once we're docked, we can go to one of the restaurants in town."

She grunted in agreement and continued below deck. For the life of her she couldn't figure him out. His moods were more sporadic than a hormonal teenager—one minute nice and the next barking orders at her like she was a prisoner on a chain gang. Shoving her negative thoughts about Damian deeply into the recesses of her mind, she stripped out of her wetsuit and clothes. *Hormonal teen or drug addict in need of a hit?* The second part of that thought gave her pause, and it would explain a whole lot of his actions since she'd met him. She decided to ask Tim if he'd seen Damian using drugs in college.

Stepping into the flow of the steaming shower, she thought about the wonderful time she'd had in the salt water on the second dive. So many beautiful colors and such fascinating life-forms. The world under the sea had so much to offer that she couldn't understand why Damian had bailed on it. Shaking her head in confusion, Willa realized that she'd rather be sharing the trip with Tim.

AFTER TROTTING BACK from the parking lot in the rain, Tim took off his wet shirt and sneakers. He heard Willa's reprimand in his head from the day he admitted to seriously disliking flip-flops. The longer he was in Banyan Tree Bay, the more the ever-present rubber foot coverings made sense. Shuddering over the idea of shoving that stupid plastic thingy between his toes, he decided to at least look for a pair of slides.

"What has become of your life, Harley? Are you really filling your mind with such inane bullshit?" As if to jog him out of the thought process, a blinding white flash of light filled the sky, instantly followed by a horrendous booming that rattled the windows of his place. Given the lack of time between the lightning and the thunder, he had to assume the storm was directly over them.

Moving to the main living area, he realized the last strike had knocked out the electricity. Groaning over the inconvenience, Tim picked up his work phone. With multiple flags showing on the face of it, he groaned even deeper, but he wasn't sure why. Three days ago, he had expected to work all weekend, deep in disaster with the tropical storm's arrival. But the lovely Gina had taken a right-hand turn and powered her way up through the center of the Atlantic Ocean, leaving them with only the possibility of thunderstorms.

With the reality of unexpected downtime upon him, Tim ignored the notifications on his phone, grabbed one of the paperbacks he had just unpacked from the shelf under the television, and settled on the couch. It was rare for him to read during the day, but he decided to lap up the time and actually take a day off.

Chapter Eighteen

After dawdling in the primary cabin for nearly an hour, Willa wasn't surprised when she heard the motors of the catamaran turn over. It's possible that Damian had gotten word about openings at the dock, or maybe he decided to move closer, hooking themselves to a mooring ball while waiting. Moving to the deck, she looked up at the flybridge before climbing the small set of steps. When she stuck her head into the control room, Damian cast a look at her.

"Sorry, I couldn't wait any longer for you. Did you use all of the hot water in the hold?" He chuckled at his absurd suggestion.

"I tried, but my skin got very shrivelly." Willa found herself rubbing her thumbs over the pads of her other digits and the top of her hands. "Between the time in the salt water and the shower, my skin was begging for moisturizer."

"No problem. We're going to move in a few minutes.

Will you please secure the food I left out on the table for you? Then when you feel me slowing down again, I'll need you to hook us to the mooring ball. I mean, assuming there is nothing available on the dock."

"Aye-aye, captain." Willa gave him a mock salute before retreating to the galley. Under the current conditions, she didn't mind Damian taking charge.

Willa felt the cat move just as she lifted the cheese plate from the table and onto the countertop where a small metal guard would keep it from falling off. Bracing her feet slightly apart, she looked at the food, which caused her stomach to rumble. She couldn't remember when she'd eaten, and her underwater time had drained any carbohydrates her body had held in reserve. Leaning forward against the cabinet, she found herself eating slice after slice of the tasty selection before the boat slowing interfered. After eating her fill, Willa guzzled a bottle of water, taking up any remaining space in her belly. Hopefully he wouldn't want to go to a restaurant very soon.

THE INCESSANT PINGING of his personal phone wouldn't go away. "For crying out loud," he shouted at the empty room as he dragged his sleepy ass off the couch to where he'd left the phone in the kitchen.

"Jerk, why wasn't it on the coffee table." The little voice inside his head responded immediately. *Because you needed the rest.* Maybe so.

Pressing his thumb to the bottom of the screen, he found three missed texts from Jenn. Glancing up at the small digits in the upper left-hand corner, he was shocked to see that it was nearly two in the morning. When he'd first awoken from the annoying sound, he thought the darkness outside his windows meant it was around ten, not four hours later. Why would Willa's friend be contacting him now?

Tim double tapped the icon, filling the screen with messages from Jenn and Monica Dearborn. "Oh shit." He swore at himself for letting the power outage caused by the storm to lull him into a sense of peace and quiet. Staring at both names, he selected his employee first. Reading from newest to oldest, he noted that the messages were spread out over a two-hour window, ending about an hour ago.

Plan on lots of action at the station tomorrow.

I know, it's Sunday.

Wright and Ortiz picked up Leon tonight on my orders.

Lots of new info on smuggling.

Sorry to bother you, chief. I need to speak to you.

. . .

TRYING to decide about contacting her immediately, Tim almost forgot about the messages from Jenn. This time he started with the oldest one, marked at nine.

Just got the weirdest texts from Willa. Forwarding to you.

Willa: Having a nice dinner at The Island Grove in St. Thomas.

Willa: Weird. Damian cut his hand in the men's room.

Willa: Men just chased us from restaurant. Trying to reach boat.

Willa: Scared.

Tim, where are you? Did you read the ones from Willa?

She isn't responding to me now.

How do we help her?

TIM??????

Not caring about the time, he pressed the small picture of a phone by her name at the top of the text. It took two rings for her to answer.

"Oh, thank God, you called me. What am I supposed to do? My friend is scared and in danger. Tim, please help. I don't know what to do." Jenn's voice pushed the edge of hysteria by the time she took a breath.

"Okay, first, hold on and let me piece this together."

"Okay." Her voice wavered with uncertainty.

"Willa and Damian were chased, or attacked, by men in some town called Charlotte Amalie tonight? And they tried to escape by running to the catamaran they were using?" About a thousand and one scenarios popped into his mind, none of them good.

A high-pitched yes squeaked through the speaker.

"I'm going to the station. I have lots of contact information there for departments in the Keys, Puerto Rico, Aruba, and the Virgin Islands."

"Can I come with you?"

Tim took a deep breath before answering her. "No, Jenn. I'm sorry—but if my instincts are correct, the station will be lit up with officers and federal officials within an hour. I think you should stay at your house." He didn't even know where her house was, but he didn't want her overhearing any conversations about jewel or drug running. At that point, he didn't even know if Willa was involved. His heart said no, she was a wonderful human. Fingers crossed she was an innocent bystander Damian had selfishly dragged into the melee.

WILLA WAS THRILLED when she realized Damian was heading to the dock. After the breakneck speed of their trip down, she really needed to spend a few pleasant hours on land. Not waiting for instructions, she ran to the portside of the boat and grabbed the bow dock line, tossing it to a man waiting for it. Then she bolted to the stern, waiting to throw the next tether to the dock hand. When Damian killed the engine, a sweet relief traveled from her neck, over her shoulders, and down her back.

She watched as he closed the flybridge, slipping the ignition key into the right-hand front pocket of his shorts. With the grace of a mountain lion, he ascended the upper deck and came to her under the hardtop of the cockpit lounge. Damian waved to another boat while sliding his left arm around her waist, pulling her in for an unexpected deep kiss. When he released her, Willa stepped back, instinctively wiping the back of her hand across her lips as her temper surged. *What was that about? Is he marking his territory? Claiming me as his?*

"I'm going down to put on something respectable." He tugged on the front of the faded T-shirt he had on. "There are some flyers in the salon—top drawer under the counter with the fruit bowl. See if you find something enticing for us to do."

He brushed a quick kiss across her forehead and stepped away as his phone pinged from somewhere in his shorts. Willa saw his brows furrow staring at the surface of the never-far-from-him contraption. Waving it at her, he looked up from his phone. "I've got a call to make. See you in a few."

When his bare feet carried him down the companionway, Willa scanned the other vessels docked near them before retrieving the papers he'd suggested she peruse. Settling into the first seat of the cockpit lounge, she dropped the used menus on the table.

"So freaking old school," she mumbled to herself and opened her cell phone. Using the map application, Willa tapped on the red dot indicating where they were, pulling up detailed information on Charlotte Amalie. From there, she clicked on the RESTAURANTS tab. As a surprisingly long list populated her screen, Willa glanced around at the sound of laughter.

Finding a group of people sitting under the hardtop of a cat two berths down the dock, she felt a sharp pang of loneliness come over her. The four couples were teasing each other, with the men taking the lead on what should be insults to each other. But no one seemed upset —instead they toasted a few times, the late sun shimmering off jewelry on the hands of the women. She thought about the times that she, Tim, and Jenn had laughed like that. Willa wished she had a large group of friends. Other than Jenn and Tim, the only people she saw on a regular basis were at Damian's watering holes.

"Hey, you're in paradise right now. Enjoy the moment." Willa whispered to herself, shaking off any melancholy that threatened her. Clicking through the list on her phone, at least six of the restaurants appealed to her. She marked each of them, wondering how much longer Damian would be.

Tired of browsing the list, she opened her favorite

social media app, getting lost in the never-ending list of inane posts about food, music, politics, and vacations. On occasion, her finger paused from flicking for her to read a highlighted quote. That's when Damian placed his hand on her shoulder, causing her to squeak in surprise.

"What do you think?" He waved to the papers on the table in front of her.

"I found a few. Have you been here, in this town, before?"

"Oh, yeah." He nodded his head sagely.

"Then how about you pick where we eat. Local mom and pops are usually a gold mine of deliciousness." She saw his eyes flicker, but he said nothing until she stood up.

"Well, that's no problem here. I'm not even sure there's a chain on the entire island." Chuckling, he pointed downward. "Things are casual around here, but you still need something on your feet."

Quickly she rummaged through the basket on the shelf between the window to the salon and the seat. Tossing a few pairs of flip-flops aside, she found the sandals she had on the day she'd come aboard the *No Bananas*. Grabbing them, she followed Damian to the dock where he held out a hand for her. Steadying herself on his strength, she took the few steps to the floating aluminum, dropped the sandals, and quickly stepped into them to prevent her feet from burning on the hot metal.

"So m'darling—" Willa giggled as Damian held his

arm across his stomach, bending at the waist. "—it is with great honor that I invite you to join me for the best tasting food on the Island of St. Thomas."

A happy smile crossed her face, releasing the tension she'd been wrapped in since leaving Banyan Tree Bay. *At last, my wonderful, badly needed vacation has begun!*

Chapter Nineteen

Willa wondered if they would die on the next turn in the ever-curving road. The older minivan flew up a hill, leaving her with only a broad expanse of ocean to see. Normally, that would please Willa, but it felt more like she was in the front car of an out-of-control roller-coaster ride. Suddenly, the driver stomped on the brakes, saying something in a thick Creole accent as she flew forward, stopping only when her shoulder smashed into the seat in front of her where Damian sat.

"Okay?" He gave her a backwards, one-handed pat on her knee.

Trying to control her temper, Willa nearly growled at him. "Yes."

At Damian's direction, the driver pulled into what the Virgin Islands considered a road. What Willa saw was a narrow path cut through a thick stand of tall, leafy shrubs that scratched the sides of the car as they flew by, wheels jolting her spine as they popped in and out of potholes.

A moment later, they came to a jolting stop in front of a single-story building that seemed to spread in every direction. One end appeared to be a hotel, while the other end had a wraparound porch nearly hidden by various sized palms.

Damian passed money to the driver and stepped out of the passenger's side, turning to open the sliding door for her. With a delicate squeeze to her hand, he pulled her to a standing position. When Willa realized he was about to kiss her, she turned her head sideways, forcing him to settle for her cheek. "Are you ready to eat?"

Willa nodded even though she had spent the ten-minute car ride wishing she hadn't eaten as much of the cheese as she had an hour before. With her fingers crossed in her head, she replied, "Ooh, smells good."

When they walked through the front door, an attractive woman greeted Damian warmly. Her smile and the kiss she planted on his lips indicated a fondness that surprised Willa and left her feeling like a third wheel. *He seems to know her. Am I stepping onto his home turf?*

"Jacqueline, this is my dear friend, Willa." He let go of the local woman to slide his arm around Willa's shoulder.

"It is a pleasure, dear. Welcome to the Island Grove." The woman extended a perfectly manicured hand to her.

"It's nice to meet you." Despite the niggling questions dancing around in her head, Willa smiled sweetly when shaking the gorgeous woman's hand.

"Damian," Jacqueline's accent pulled the last two letters into three, sounding like *-yon*. I have your table ready."

As she led them through the crowded room, the woman seemed to float rather than walk. Her supple light brown skin giving her an exotic air. The more Willa saw of the apparent maître de, the more she noticed an obvious intimacy with Damian.

As they passed through the larger seating area, Willa was surprised when the woman finally stopped at a lace-covered, single table in a private room. Now that they were out of the discord of other dinner guests, strains of soft calypso music reached her ears as a waiter held her chair. When they were both seated, Jacqueline placed her hand on Damian's shoulder while casting a smile that didn't reach her eyes in Willa's direction. "Marcus will be taking care of you tonight." After a three second kiss to Damian's lips—which was two seconds longer than Willa thought necessary—she left them alone with the waiter.

Why is this bothering you so much? You know how much you've been thinking about Tim and moving on. And guess what? The answer is yes. Damian and this woman are bed buddies. But, before you lose your temper, just remember that you are far from home. Not exactly out of your element, but totally dependent upon him. She glanced at Damian, who appeared oblivious to the anger filling her head. *If you try to leave, you won't even know if the taxi will take you in the correct direction.*

Deciding to make the best of the trip, Willa slapped down the conversation in her head. But there was no denying to herself that she was through with this relationship. At this point, she was doing her best to keep the peace with Damian until he got her home, with her trust hanging on by a tenuous thread.

"Everything they make is delicious."

Looking up at him when she felt Damian's hand on hers, she found the adorable surfer-dude smile that originally attracted her to him.

"What's your favorite?"

"Oh, boy. Tough call. But probably the Jamaican pork stew."

"Okay, that's what I will have." She smiled at him, hoping he didn't detect anything awry.

Once they had given their order to Marcus, Damian raised his glass of wine in a toast. "To traveling with the beautiful woman in my life."

Willa gave the rim of his glass a gentle tap of her own. "Here's to a lovely trip." After that, they fell into a deep conversation about the fish they had seen when snorkeling, the increased number of lionfish, and the pristine waters. Considering the number of people seated in the front room, and the orders ahead of theirs, she was surprised when their food quickly arrived at their table.

When the rich scents of ginger, thyme, and allspice reached her nose, Willa completely forgot about being nauseous from too much cheese and bad driving. Instead, she took to her dish like a lost sailor who had been floating at sea for days, enjoying the way the sticky white rice calmed the heat of the Scotch bonnet peppers. After a few minutes, she heard Damian give a soft chuckle.

"They're not going to take it away from you."

The heat of embarrassment flushed Willa's face. "I know. But it's good. And I'm hungry." She speared another piece of the cubed pork and put it into her mouth, ending any further discussion. When Marcus came back to ask about dessert, she didn't give Damian's judgmental comment any consideration.

"I'll have the red grout."

The waiter smiled at her choice. "You will enjoy that very much. It's a signature dish here in the Virgin Islands."

"Great, thank you." Willa noticed that Damian declined any dessert and ordered a double shot of Pusser's Rum on ice. Looking at the half-empty glass of wine at her place, her first in several days, she had wondered how long it would be before he hit the local preference. Expecting him to continue on with multiple rounds of the rum, she was happy there were no obvious car rental locations at the marina, and that they had taken a cab. No way would she want him behind the wheel, and she wasn't comfortable with being the driver with how cavalier the locals appeared to be.

Before she could overthink Damian's alcohol consumption, Marcus returned with the small dish of local delight. It had been many years since Willa had been near the Caribbean and access to this treasure. With the first spoonful of tapioca, guava, and sweet Danish vanilla ice cream, her taste buds seemed to do a thank you dance on her tongue. The competing textures, along with the rich, creamy sweetness of the ice cream caused her to moan with delight, threatening to give her an epicurean orgasm.

But her intense pleasure ceased when Damian scraped his chair along the wooden floor and stood up. "Men's room. I'll be back in a moment." Willa didn't bother responding with more than a slight nod.

When she finished the island treat, she realized that Damian had been away from the table for more than the moment he had suggested. With no reason to worry, she continued to enjoy the solace.

Running her tongue along the surface of her lips, Willa discovered the remnants of the sweet red grout. As the soft music wrapped around her, finding the decadent dessert still on her lips led her to evocative thoughts about Tim, especially the taste of his kiss just hours before she began the trip. Remembering how he traced her lips with his tongue, how he held her safely in his strong arms, and the concern in his eyes as they separated. Willa found herself deep in thought when she heard a noise coming from the back of the restaurant.

Seriously, where did he go?

When Damian burst around the corner holding his right hand tight to his belly, his eyes wide with what looked to be shock, Willa vaulted from the table to meet him. Consumed with guilt, she tried to move his arm. “What is wrong Damian?”

“Nothing. Let’s go. NOW!” His barking order slapped her in the face as he grabbed her with his free hand and propelled her toward the door.

“But Damian.” Her words were sliced by his deep voice.

“Shut up. We’re leaving.”

She managed to stay upright and moving despite the force of his hand at her back and the pulsing fear that consumed her.

“DEARBORN, UPDATE, STAT!” Tim’s shout echoed across the near-empty squad room to Monica’s open door on his way to his office, ignoring the surprised looks on the faces of his staff. *What, you’ve never seen the chief walk in at three in the morning?* He tried to tone down the snarky voice in his head. Just because he had emotional skin in the game didn't mean they became his punching bags.

Trying to curry favor, he swung through the break room to make fresh coffee. Tapping his right foot while he waited for the dark nectar to brew, he looked around the space. Ironically, the set up was almost identical to the one in his precinct in Albany. Pursing his lips, he wondered why he hadn't slowed down enough since arriving in Banyan Tree Bay to notice the similarity. Tim filled his cup and met the special investigator in his office.

"Sorry about that, I'm cranky." He waved for her to take a seat. "Please, sit."

"Thank you, boss. Do you want to read through this, or shall I give you the CliffsNotes?"

Tim couldn't believe how the physical file had grown in the two days since he'd last seen it. "No doubt, CliffsNotes, please."

"Based upon research done in the last twenty-four hours by Wright and Ortiz, Leon Graves and Damian Buck are both working for Michael Lyons at Islands & More Water Adventures. They haul several different drugs and styles of gemstones from various islands in the Caribbean. The pickup points are as close to the mainland U.S as the Major Antilles and as far away as St. John in the USVI. Leon's recent trip was to Mastic Point, North Andros, Bahamas, that's why he was back so soon. Buck, on the other hand, was scheduled for St. John."

Tim's mind flashed back to the text Willa had sent to Jenn.

> Having a nice dinner at the Island Grove in St. Thomas.
>
> Weird. Damian cut his hand in the men's room.
>
> Men just chased us from restaurant. Trying to reach boat.
>
> Scared.

What were they doing on St. Thomas when his pickup was supposed to be in St. John?

"How about Lyons at the port? Any idea who's pulling his strings?

"Yes, sir. That was the next set of notes."

He looked up to see Dearborn suppressing a laugh at her commanding officer. When he didn't interrupt her, she flipped another page in the report and started reading.

"Michael Lyons, who, by the way, is from Long Island and a territorial leader for Dominick Pasternova, a known mob boss and drug lord in—"

Tim raised his hand before she could continue.

"I'm quite familiar with Pasternova and his operation." *I just never thought Damian was stupid enough to get caught up in the lifestyle.*

"Sir, Pasternova has a lengthy list of missing mules."

Tim gave her a single nod in acknowledgment.

"Buck seems to have kept his nose clean for a while, probably not in any danger from the family."

Tim kept his face devoid of emotion. None of his staff knew about his arm's-length relationship with Damian.

"Also, sir, lots of recent chatter in the islands about the alleged discovery of a Spanish ship in the water off the western end of St. Thomas. In American waters. Things are pretty hush-hush about the exact location, but rumor has it that old coins from the ship are showing up at a few antiquities dealers."

"Are those dealers in the islands or here on the mainland?"

"Mostly down there but a handful have been received at a business in Naples, sir."

"Thanks Monica." As she stood, he extended his hand, "I'll take the hard copy so I can read through it before I call the commissioner in a few hours."

He stared at the dog-eared manilla folder, wondering if Damian's family had the power and the money to bail him out of this, assuming he made it back to the States alive.

Knowing it was too early to call his brother, Tim sent him a brief text.

Call me when you get this.

Expecting to hear from John around five thirty, Tim concentrated on absorbing two inches of printed out information before then.

WITH DAMIAN'S hand still pushing her, they crossed the dark parking lot and started down the makeshift driveway. Every few feet Willa felt her knees and hips buckle when her foot landed in an unexpected pothole. With needles of pain ricocheting through her lower body, she squinted through the darkness, hoping to avoid further injury. When they finally stepped out on the macadam, they were nearly mown down by a passing truck, highlighting their newest problem: navigating the narrow road in the dark while avoiding the erratic local driving habits.

Willa took out her cell phone, intent upon using the flashlight app when possible.

Damian wrenched it from her hands. "No calls. No texts."

Does he know you texted Tim earlier?

With a sudden burst of rage, she slapped him across the face, and grabbed it back from him. "Who do you think you are?"

"Willa, you don't understand. These people aren't playing. Now put the phone away until we get down there." He pointed to a lit-up building about half a mile down the hill.

"Not even the flashlight?"

Shaking his head, his silhouette seemed to be leaning more to his right. "Sorry." His voice had softened.

The heavy weight of fear landed in her stomach, threatening everything she had just eaten. But, based upon how poor he was looking and sounding, she wouldn't ask any questions until they were on the boat.

Stepping up their pace to jog, Willa and Damian made good time in between passing vehicles. Arriving at the building much sooner than she expected, he pulled her to the side of the apparent store.

"Please go inside here. To your right should be a bulletin board of sorts. You'll find a few business cards there. Hopefully one is a cab company. Hurry." But before she could leave, he grabbed her arm. "Don't speak to anyone. Just bring the card out. They don't need to hear your accent."

She shivered as goose bumps covered her arms, her mind trying to protect her from the depth of the danger they were in. "You can kick his ass later. For now, let's do this," she whispered to herself as she walked to the front door.

When she entered the store, the few people standing in line at the register made her feel conspicuous, and guilty. But their attention on her lasted just a few seconds as the first man in line was handed his change and left. In the minute it took for her to locate the business listings Damian had mentioned, the store had cleared, leaving her for the owner to scrutinize. Even though she had the card in her pocket, she traced her fingers over a few of the listings, intentionally shaking her head no.

"You need help with something?"

Willa shook her head after the owner's voice made her jump slightly. Not wanting to spike his curiosity as she moved toward the door, Willa began mocking the man in Thai. In her head she was laughing with her maternal grandfather over her telling the store owner he was a fool and likes to pry into the affairs of the villagers.

Chapter Twenty

Once past the glow of the light over the doorway, Willa dashed around the building to find Damian sitting at the base of the block wall.

"Are you okay?" She automatically placed her hand on his forehead to check for a fever, but his skin was cool to the touch.

"Cab?" He pointed to the card she had pulled from her pocket.

"Yeah." With shaking hands, she dialed the ten digits and waited for an answer. When a deeply accented female voice answered, Willa struggled to maintain her composure.

"Cab, please."

"Pickup location?"

Rattled by the question, Willa trotted a few steps toward the road so she could see the front of the building. "Two. Nine. One. Eatate."

"Northside then, mum?"

"I believe so."

"Ten minutes. Be ready."

Willa was about to let out a relieved breath when she saw a sedan moving slowly down the same hill she and Damian had just walked. She watched them for a minute before she realized there was a single beam of light coming from within the car, sweeping the sides of the road. She didn't know what had happened back at the restaurant, but her spidey-sense jacked into gear at the sight of that small light.

She raced to Damian's side thankful she hadn't encouraged him to move from his place in the shadows. "Dame. Dame." Willa covered his mouth with her left hand and held her right index finger over her lips. In a raspy whisper, she answered the question in his eyes. "I think someone followed us."

Damian shook his head at her while pushing her hand away from his mouth. "Not good."

"We have about five more minutes before the cab gets here. Hopefully they're gone by then." When the crunching sound of car tires crossing gravel filled the quiet night, Willa pinned her body to the block wall and slowly slid to sit by Damian.

The vehicle slowed as the bright headlights swept the area in an arc. *They must be turning around.* When the motion stopped, Willa could hear the soft ticking of an engine in need of oil while the narrow light traveled along the ground in the dense plants.

With each of them drawing shallow breaths, she glanced at the small trees and unkempt shrubs they were sitting in. If ever she needed a guardian angel, tonight was it.

When the sound of the tires changed from crushing gravel to the smooth surface of asphalt, Willa stood up. Pushing Damian's hand from her wrist, she sprinted to the edge of the shadows to catch the taillights of the car pulling away.

"They're gone," she whispered to him once she'd returned to the shadows. But no sooner had she said it than she heard another car slowly crossing the gravel lot as her phone pinged. Taking a risk, she looked around the block corner, relieved to see an older model compact with familiar numbers written on the side.

Pulling Damian to his feet, Willa draped his good arm over her shoulder, guiding him in the dark so he wouldn't trip. When she yanked open the back door of the cab, relief over no inside light to illuminate their faces nearly swamped her. Moments later, she gave the driver the address for Crown Bay Marina.

Willa struggled to quell her fears, surrounded by darkness, and crammed into the back seat with Damian. With each pitch, quick start, and jerking stop, she was sure she would never see Tim, her family, or friends like Jenn again. She didn't know what Damian had gotten her into, but her deepest, internal sense told her their lives were in danger. Using a game to control her thoughts about dying, Willa filled her mind with life in

Banyan Tree Bay, making it seem like no time had passed when the cabbie slammed on the brakes and spun into the affluent marina, waving to the armed guard at the gate.

Willa waited until Damian was walking away from the battered cab before she tapped the driver on the shoulder. When he turned from watching Damian's crooked gait to look at her, she saw questions in his eyes.

"Shh." She held her finger up in front of the man's face. "Don't mention this." In response to his blinking lashes, Willa stuffed three twenty-dollar bills into the driver's hands even though his meter only displayed the number eighteen. He nodded quickly as she slid out the door. Without looking back, she trotted a few steps to Damian's side, hoping the man never spoke about the fare.

"WHAT'S GOING ON?"

"Hey, thanks for calling." Tim was relieved to hear his brother's voice.

"Is everything okay?"

John's question bounced in his head. Tim knew he could handle the case on his own, but it would go faster and cleaner with John's help.

"Yeah. I'm fine. But this case is not."

He could hear John making coffee in the background. A moment later, his sister-in-law chimed in.

"'Morning, Tim. How's the weather down there?"

Part of him wanted to despise her for the cheery lilt of her voice, but the other part of him knew that optimism was one of Kara's strongest characteristics.

"Ha. Pretty hot and sticky yesterday when some storms rolled through."

"Oh, my favorite twin brother-in-law." Her chuckle rumbled through the speaker. "You're the one who needed to get as far away as possible, but still stay in the same time zone."

"Thanks for that, Irish."

"Sorry to cut you off, I hear the kids fussing. Enjoy your chat with John."

Tim thought he heard a young voice in the background just as his brother took over.

"Hey, you've got about five minutes of my undivided attention. What's up?"

Tim rattled off the extreme fast forward on Damian, drugs, diamonds, Spanish coins, and the Pasternova connection, wrapping it up with a single question. "How soon can you get here?"

"I'll call you back in five."

Tim knew he was asking a lot of his brother, and his family. But if John could spare less than a week tapping his connections while Tim and his crew worked theirs, the entire investigation could be ready to hand off to the feds a lot sooner and a lot cleaner. He just hoped John would come. As if their twin telepathy really existed, Tim's phone lit up with John's name.

"Around six tonight. Text me your address."

"I can pick you up at the airport, you know."

"Nah. I'll need a car to get around, anyway."

"Okay, see you later. And John? Thanks." Tim suspected this was a bad time for John to be away from their family business. Even though it was ninety degrees in Banyan Tree Bay, it was early fall in upstate New York, and it attracted a whole lot of farm stand activity and leaf peepers. But more importantly, it was the start of fox hunting season, Kara's latest adventure.

"No problem. Gotta run, I haven't been out to the kennel yet and the flight leaves in three hours."

Tim thought about the melee that awaited his brother. Nearly thirty happy, healthy, and vociferous, Labrador retrievers and foxhounds would be racing around in their generously sized outdoor pens demanding breakfast.

WITH THE *NO Bananas* docked less than thirty yards away, Willa hoped she and Damian had made it to safety. In her mind, they would head into the salon, lock everything behind them, and sail out tomorrow morning after a good night's sleep.

But Damian had other ideas, expressing them as soon as they reached the cat. "Untie both ends while I go up to start the engines." He pointed to either end of the boat.

"Wait. You're injured." She couldn't believe he wanted to leave the dock.

"Willa." Damian pulled her closer to him. "This is my boat. I am the captain. I will make the decisions." His voice had dropped an octave and gained a severe edge she'd never heard before. "If you're going with me, get those fucking ropes off of those cleats and onto this vessel, along with your ass." He hobbled up the dockside steps and then the portside steps to the flybridge before turning around to growl at her. "Now."

Darting to the front of the boat, she unwrapped the dock rope as quickly as she could in the weak lighting. Trying to ignore a commotion in the parking lot, Willa ran to the stern end and squatted at the cleat. With just two more serpentines of the rope remaining to free the *No Bananas*, Damian started the engines. With the water under the dock bubbling to life, Willa shot up the portable steps and up to the flybridge.

Sliding in next to Damian, she pointed to where a crowd had gathered around the guard shack. Blue and red lights bounced off the shiny white fiberglass of many of the boats in the marina, with the distinct blaring of sirens drowning out all other sounds. After watching for less than thirty seconds, Damian shook his head at her, pressing his index finger over his lips. Then he gave her a reassuring squeeze of her shoulder before sliding the cat into reverse. Willa remained pinned to his side until they were floating in the dark water of Baye de Grigri.

"I need your help with something." Damian turned off the motors and started down the stairs, but Willa had yet to move. "Please." Even though she couldn't see his face in the moonless night sky, she thought she heard a difference in his voice.

"Sure. I'll be right there." She waited a moment and picked her way to the salon, arriving just as he unlocked the sliding glass door. Willa stepped into the air-conditioned space and let out a deep breath. Gazing at the padded banquette seats, Willa felt like she'd been gone for days, when it had only been a few hours. Her exhausted body begged her to lay down immediately. But her worried mind knew she needed to have a conversation with Damian before she could truly rest.

Hearing him return to the salon from the primary cabin, Willa looked up to see him carrying medical supplies. "What's all that for?" Without a word, he dropped the supplies on the table and held up his shirt, exposing a gaping wound on his right side.

"Oh my God. What happened to you?" She tried to suppress an ear-piercing scream; afraid someone would hear her.

"It's a long story. Can you just clean me up?" He shook his head and let out a long, slow breath. "I'll fill you in on the details tomorrow when I know we're out of danger."

"Oh, Damian. What have you gotten us into?" Not expecting an answer, Willa tore open the package of small gauze pads, saturating a handful with peroxide before touching him.

WHEN WILLA WOKE UP, she could feel the *No Bananas* clipping through water at a high pace. She slid out of bed, padding to the bathroom. Even though she'd taken a shower before falling asleep, the urge to take another was overwhelming. After using the toilet, she dropped her lightweight pajamas on the floor and stepped into the driving pulse of steaming water, trying to wash the sight of Damian's torn flesh from her mind.

She was an artist, not a nurse or doctor. She didn't want the ugliness of his injury to have permanent residence in her mind. If she was honest, she didn't want any thoughts of this miserable weekend trip to remain with her. Damian's moodiness was enough of a turn off. But when added to how mean he could be, and then the danger of last night, Willa couldn't wait to be back in Banyan Tree Bay, ignoring him.

Even though she tried, she wasn't even a very good first mate. If she were, wouldn't she have gone topside when she awoke to check on things? Instead, she was using countless gallons of steaming freshwater, hiding in the shower, pretending this was all a bad dream.

"Pull yourself together, chick. Since when does self-pity get anything accomplished other than giving yourself a headache?" Turning off the water, she rung the moisture from her hair as best she could. Once she left the confined space of the head, she ran a dry towel over her body and then rolled her hair into a turban on top of her skull. A baby-sized giggle escaped her lips thinking about how many times she'd done that with her hair. A classic action for women with more than shoulder length hair.

Applying a thick layer of shea butter to her arms and legs, she felt the urge to giggle return. *What is wrong with me? None of this is funny.* Feeling slightly lightheaded, she sat on the bed, closed her eyes, and dropped her hands to the mattress to either side of her hips. As her chest tightened and pain filled her lungs, Willa realized she was having a panic attack. It had been so many years since she'd had one that she wrestled with her memory as the pain increased.

She sucked in a long, deep breath and began counting. F-i-v-e Slowly she let out her breath as she looked around the room, counting objects—the mirror, her hairbrush, Damian's unused pillow, her phone resting on the bed, the handle on the diminutive closet door. F-o-u-r. She touched the blanket, her hair, the container of shea butter leaning on her thigh, and her pillow. T-h-r-e-e. She heard the water slapping on the pontoon, the second hand of the clock on the nightstand, the water dripping in the shower. T-w-o. She could smell the fresh lotion on her skin, and the conditioner in her hair as the turban fell down her shoulder. O-n-e. She could taste the fresh mint toothpaste she had just used.

Willa gazed at herself in the mirror hanging on the back of the cabin door. Vignettes of her mother crossed her mind repeatedly. Lilly Davidson was incredibly beautiful, artistic, and courageous. With her mother's love supporting her, Willa decided that she had the strength to deal with Damian despite his shadowy lifestyle. All she needed to do was get home to Banyan Tree Bay, then she would walk away from him.

For weeks Willa suspected that Damian didn't fit into the life of a mature woman. Yeah, sure, he appealed to the scant smidgen of what remained of twenty-year-old Willa, but not to the woman she'd grown into. Knowing she wanted to get home and walk away from her surfer-dude experiment, Willa pulled on a sports bra and panties, covered by a tank top and shorts. Gone were the unfettered D-cups she had dangled in front of him for two days while she mistakenly thought she wanted this to be a romantic trip. In their place was the businesswoman who cleared seven figures annually.

Standing from the bed, she fluffed her loose tresses with the towel and then began to brush them. As she ran the hard plastic teeth through the strands of black and chestnut, she thought about her well-lit and inviting apartment over her shop. Banyan Tree Bay was the place where she had grown from a raging young warrior who tussled with her siblings into a successful businesswoman. It was the place where she'd built her life, her friendships, and her reputation for over twenty years. And she was not allowing him to keep her away from there any longer.

Chapter Twenty-One

By the time Willa made it to the cockpit, the Sunday morning sun had risen fully, casting a million flickering diamonds across the surface of the ocean. Despite the speed they traveled, she was still able to see deep into the turquoise waters. Off the starboard side of the cat, she watched a school of dolphins tagging along with them, leaping to the surface and whistling to each other. Without question, the southern waters were spectacular, and the playful dolphins were just what Willa needed to see to tamp down the sadness in her heart.

"Good morning." She'd moved so quietly that Damian looked surprised to see her.

"Hi. Sleep well?" He shook his head at the cup of coffee she offered.

"Yes, thanks. How's your side?" She took the liberty of lifting his T-shirt, relieved to find no new bleeding.

"Fine." He pushed her hand away. "Can you handle this?"

"What? Skippering?" A simple nod was his only response. "Matter of fact, I can. Go get some sleep." Willa was surprised by how ragged he looked—dark circles under his eyes, sallow skin, with deep lines etched into his forehead and around his eyes.

"We'll need fuel in about two hours. I planned on stopping at Matthew Town on the west side of Big Inagua Island. After that, we'll track northeast and then stay east of Ragged Island and that strip of Cays. After that, if we need it again, we'll stop for fuel at the first spot we can on the east side of the big island in the Bahamas. It's a little out of our way but we can scoot back around the southern tip to open water."

"Go. I'll be okay." Willa pointed to the portside flybridge doorway.

Before he moved, Damian leaned down to her, brushing his dry lips across hers, leaving a trace of salt.

"Drink some water before you crash."

He waved over his head as he made his way below deck.

Man, he must be tired. He left me in charge but doesn't even know that I am experienced at this. And she had no intention of telling him. Whatever this crashing-mad-dash of a weekend truly was, every bit of it was his fault and there was no way she was bailing him out by splitting the driving in half. She would only do it for a few hours since she had no interest in dying in a boat wreck.

Willa took in the massive expanse of water, making herself comfortable in the flybridge with her coffee, yogurt, and cheese sticks. As the depths below the catamaran changed, so did the color of the water. From a light turquoise to a deep blue and even nearly black, the sea was an artist's dream. Once she'd finished the first cup of joe, she pulled out her cell phone. No, the pictures wouldn't be the best, but she'd still be able to capture the swirling colors to look at later. Just because the romance was over for her concerning Damian, it didn't mean her internal painter couldn't benefit from being surrounded by such beauty.

As she looked from side to side with nothing but open water in her sights, Willa let her mind travel to more thoughts of Tim. The first one to pop up was the discussion they'd had about flip-flops. He'd been so staid, yet hilarious, about the negative aspects of wearing the ever-present beach gear. Until that evening, she'd never given a thought to flip-flops. In her mind, they just existed. Thinking about the simplicity of their laughter warmed Willa's heart, filling her face with a smile.

With her thoughts skittering between Tim, painting, and hurricane season, over ninety minutes had flown by when Willa felt the autopilot adjusting the catamaran's speed. She'd found such pleasure in watching the sea that she even forgot the boat was set on an assist. She couldn't help but laugh thinking of her dad and what he would have thought of this sort of contraption.

"What's so funny?"

At the sound of Damian's voice she jumped from the

comfortable bench, clutching the small revolver next to her. The one she'd slipped in her bag before leaving Banyan Tree Bay. "Oh, for Christ's sake."

Damian held his hands up. "Whoa, just me. Not a pirate." He wore a crooked smile for a second and then dropped his hand. "Where'd you get that thing from, anyway?"

"Have I asked you any questions?"

"Um, no. But I get the feeling you'd like to." He flipped a few switches on the control panel without looking at her.

"There's plenty of time for that later. Apparently, your plans are to keep moving all day."

"Just remember, Annie Oakley, a moving target is harder to hit."

SINCE IT WAS STILL RELATIVELY early in the day, and there were fewer vessels coming in, the entire refueling had taken less than an hour. Willa really wanted to leave the boat to stretch her legs but decided Damian might leave without her if she wasn't there when the tanks were full. Instead, she entertained herself by cooking some breakfast while the boat was motionless.

When Damian told the dock crew it was time to push off, Willa did a quick sweep of the galley, throwing any loose dishes or implements into the sink. Knowing it would be five minutes or so before they would be up to speed, Willa decided to sit under the hardtop with a bottle of water, watching the other vessels they passed in relative obscurity.

Just as the *No Bananas* hit open water, Damian increased the throttle rapidly. The quick thrust nearly tossed her to the floor as she stepped through the sliding glass door to the salon. Gripping the edge of the counter, Willa heard something shift in the starboard side cabinet over the coffee pot. With the patience of an owl, she waited until the boat was sailing across the glass-like sea before getting up to investigate.

When she lowered the levered door of the overhead cabinet, an assortment of magazines and small books bombarded Willa's head. "Oh, shit," she squeaked and stepped aside to avoid further injury. "What the hell?" She looked down at the pile strewn about the salon floor. Moving as quickly as she was able, she scooped them up two and three at a time, dumping them on the table to organize by size. Looking at the pile, she realized there was an unusually sized object in between the layers of glossy paper.

Tossing the top layer of magazines aside, Willa found a soft leather drawstring pouch holding something loose. Lifting it with one hand, the bag was surprisingly heavy for its size. And the loose contents made a plinking sound the way a large handful of coins would. Knowing that Damian had obviously stashed this in what he must have considered a hiding spot, she didn't want him to see her with it.

Leaving the leather prize on the table, Willa took the starboard steps to the flybridge until she could see him. Relief flooded through her when she saw his right hand resting on the steering wheel, indicating that the cat was running in manual mode, and he was unlikely to move from the bench seat.

"Hey, you need anything?" She shouted her question over the splashing sound of the boat cutting through the minscule waves.

Turning to look at her, he smiled and held a canned energy drink in the air. "Nope. I'm good."

"Okay, just checking. I'll be working on some sketches." Willa pointed directly below to the salon and backed down the textured fiberglass steps. Once she knew he couldn't see her, Willa pounced on the bag, pouring its gritty contents out on the table.

"Holy cra—, " she caught herself before he could hear her shocked words. Laying on a frayed copy of *Sailing* magazine were what appeared to be ancient gold coins. Ten of them. With their surface mostly covered in dried ocean floor debris, each of them had a space the size of her pinky nail cleaned to the metal.

Willa leaned back on the banquette seating, sure that these were the reason for Damian's bullet wound. Fortunately for him, someone was a bad shot and had only grazed his side. Unfortunately for them both, these coins looked so old that she was sure no one was going to let him get away with stealing them.

Willa stared at the coins for a few minutes before her

logical side took over. Smoothing the coins out across the tattered literature, she made two rows of five with half of them face up. First, she took multiple pictures of them like that. Then she picked up the cleanest one to get a batter shot of the edge, what she thought might be a date, and the depictions under the hardened crud on either side.

"What are you doing?" Damian's voice boomed as he grabbed her upper arm, ripping her away from the table, dragging her thighs over the hard edge as he flung her out of the salon.

Willa found her footing as quickly as possible. Pissed at herself for being careless about listening for him, she needed a way to cover her tracks. "Damian, don't hurt me." She rubbed her arm even though it was the abrasion on her upper thighs that stung. "I just wanted to have a picture so I can paint them later."

"Forget about it, Willa. Why were you snooping through my shit?" His eyes sparked with the heat of his rage. "Can't you just be like any other woman and go lay in the sun?"

"Look, Damian. I didn't go looking for them. I heard something shift when you slammed it into full throttle. I was afraid it might be an open jar of some kind of fluid. I mean this is the kitchen, right?" She held her arms out, her hands tipped to the side to indicate a question. "I just wanted to make sure nothing was leaking up there. But I pulled down the door and it all just flew out onto the floor. I was picking it up."

Damian's piercing eyes held her prisoner for a moment, as if he were assessing her explanation for its veracity. Saying nothing, he slid the coins into their soft leather protection and shoved the pouch into his pocket. Without acknowledging her words, or the haphazard pile of magazines and papers, he grabbed a bottle of water from the small refrigerator and stomped away.

Willa choked on the need to laugh at the ineffective sound his bare feet made on the fiberglass surface of the boat. They both were already so close to the edge of breaking down she wasn't sure if she was containing a burst of humor, or if her anxiety had already blown to a level she didn't know how to handle.

TIM DIDN'T REALIZE how much he longed for New York, his family, and his friends until his twin brother stood in his doorway. No handshakes for these two, they pulled each other into a bear hug, not breaking the contact for almost a minute.

"It's good to see you."

Tim nodded at John, pointing for him to head upstairs instead of speaking since he didn't trust his emotions not to embarrass him. When he was hidden behind his brother's retreating back, Tim answered. "Wow, great to see you, too. Thanks for coming."

Once John had settled his belongings into the spare room, he sat at the table with Tim, accepting an ice-cold bottle of IPA. “Damn, those jeans were hot. How do you live down here?”

“If I’m not working, I wear shorts.” Tim tugged on the lightweight fabric he was in. And I bought a few pairs of slacks that feel like linen. After two days, there was no way I was going to keep wearing the khakis or denim I used to live in.”

“Fortunately for me, I’m not officially working.” John filled the open floor plan layout with a joy that Tim hadn’t felt since Willa had climbed into that catamaran with Damian. When his laugh faded, he tapped the cover of the BTBPD folder in front of them. “What’s up with this monstrosity?”

“Should we get dinner first, or order pizza? There’s plenty of beer.”

“Oh, pizza for sure.”

Tim picked up his phone and did some tapping with his index finger and credit card. Seconds later, he pulled two fresh bottles from the fridge, content to stay in with privacy instead of looking around a restaurant to see who was listening.

COUNTLESS HOURS after Damian reprimanded her, Willa watched the seemingly never-ending sunshine begin to fade. Weary from stress, she longed for a lingering, soapy bath and twelve hours in her own bed. After the disastrous foray, she swore to herself that she would never travel with a man again. Never again.

"Much longer?" Willa made sure she asked her question using a soft and inviting tone, not something more accusatory.

"'Bout two hours."

Shaking her head at his clipped response, Willa returned to the salon on her way below deck. Grabbing a lightweight, but long-sleeved, shirt, Willa returned to the stern deck to watch the sunset. She always marveled at the burst of romance she felt at this nightly ritual. Her heart pined for Tim to share it with. Not just on the boat, but every night. Her shoulders craved the pressure of his arm wrapped around them. She wanted him to pull her close, kiss her temple lightly, and tell her how beautiful she was. Yeah, it was just a fantasy—but when Willa looked to her left to see who the strong person was keeping her safe on this unknown expedition, her eyes landed on the dark hair and deep blue eyes of Tim Harley.

"Christ, you must be exhausted." With the subliminal game her mind was playing, Willa shook her head slowly at how much she missed the Yankee cop and wanted to be home with him, in Banyan Tree Bay.

Chapter Twenty-Two

John reviewed the file while eating cold pizza and listening to Tim's recap of conversations he'd had with the commissioner. From Tim's perspective, the time spent together the night before was not a waste of energy.

Looking at his phone, both men were to meet Theo Rivers at his office in city hall. Tim knew it was a risk to blindside the commissioner with the suggestion that John act as a consultant, but he thought the New York BCI connection would make it an easy sell.

As he slid into the driver's side of his Jeep, Tim looked at John.

"What are you chewing on?" His brother tapped the side of his head when he asked the question.

Apparently, I need to work on my poker face. "I was calculating the odds of you and me driving back to New York rather than you flying home, alone."

"And that's supposed to mean that you're nervous about getting fired?"

"Well, I did just show you confidential BTBPD records before securing a consultant gig for you."

John gave him one of those half-smiles the women had always swooned over. "You know what Tim? You've got a year's hold on that job in Albany. If this administration isn't smart enough to recognize how much work you have put in with your team, then they haven't earned the privilege of having you run this force."

"Thanks for your support."

"Now, don't go getting all soft on me. If you do get fired, you're driving back by yourself. I have a perfectly good, fully paid for flight that will get me there in three hours, not three days."

Both men were still laughing when Tim parked on the deserted street in front of city hall. As he glanced around the mostly commercial neighborhood, he thought it was funny that it turned into the same style of ghost town as Albany did on a Sunday.

WHEN THE HARLEY brothers returned to the street less than an hour later, John clapped him on the shoulder. "You owe me some grub."

"And I know just the place." His first thought was to take him to the fish restaurant on the outskirts of town that Willa had introduced him to. Flying by the seat of his proverbial pants, Tim hoped he would recognize the exit she had used the night they went to Isla del Sol Tenue on her sexy Moto Guzzi.

Tim was busy telling John about the beach and how it was legally a part of Banyan Tree Bay, when they pulled into the parking lot. John gave him the same reaction that Tim had given Willa when she filled him in. Fortunately, they were able to find a private table at the far end of the deck. With a strong breeze coming off the Gulf, the warm ocean water slapped the pilings underneath them, giving their conversation another level of confidentiality.

"Hey, before you introduce me to your crew tomorrow, can you give me a run-down of the sweep you're going to do?" John palmed a massive glass of ice water while he spoke.

"Sure." Tim leaned forward, resting his head in his hands, massaging his temples for a moment while he enjoyed the stress relief of Theo's immediate agreement to have John on board. "We'll take the same investigators who were on the original sweep but keep a couple of patrol cars on standby in the far corner of the parking lot. The owner's out of town right now so I don't see an issue with fanning out all over the marina at Islands & More. Even though the business is closed for the holiday, there is complete access to the docks to accommodate private vessel owners."

"What guy who owns a marina on the Gulf of Mexico shuts down for the final weekend of summer and goes out of town?"

"Ha, ha." Tim loved the snarky look on his brother's face. "I guess it's the same guy who uses said marina as a false front to a smuggling business. Kind of like those fake three-story facades you see on the recording sets of spaghetti westerns." He stopped talking when the server arrived with round one of "The Harley Boys eat all the fish in the Sea."

"Anyway, according to the marina logs, Damian's due in around nineteen hundred hours so we'll need to get in there quickly and quietly before three. Sounds like a long wait but it gives anyone watching a chance to forget seeing a few random people boarding boats owned by Lyons. Hopefully, we won't be too late, or the team will be pretty hangry."

John burst out laughing. "What are you, their mother? Give 'em a few Slim Jims and tell 'em to pace themselves."

"If we don't have sighting of him by twenty-three hundred, I'll ask for volunteers to stake it out all night. Who doesn't love overtime, right?"

Tim hoped the entire sweep was over by midnight, allowing his crew to get some rest since the operation had already shredded most of their holiday weekend.

"Tell me more about the girl," John said as he peeled the skins off a dozen steamed shrimp.

"What do you want to know? It'd be a whole lot easier if you just asked me questions."

"It's not like you to step on toes so she must be pretty special."

Tim looked up to see his brother staring at him. And John was right, he'd always made it a practice to stay out of other people's relationships. "She's smart, bossy, artistic, and funny. That's her gallery right next to my apartment." He paused a moment thinking about Willa, hoping that she would arrive back tomorrow without injury.

"And I thin—"

"That you're sweet on her?" John jumped right over him and dropped his question in the middle of the table, where it bounced around like a loose beachball.

"What? No. I was going to say that I think she's wasted on Damian. He doesn't seem to appreciate her strong traits."

"But you do, of course." John leaned back in his chair, his laugh floating halfway across the now busy deck. "If you ask me, Mrs. Harley's widdle boy has a crush on a pretty girl."

Tim considered throwing something at his brother but as twins, they already created enough of a stir when they were together. John's wife always said it was because they were as sexy AF. Women drooled and men were jealous...except those who were also drooling over the well-built Irishmen.

He took John's teasing in stride, scooped up the check, and headed toward the door, contemplating the revenge he would deliver to John later.

IT WAS close to eleven that night when Damian slowed the *No Bananas* near the northeastern corner of the big island of Bahama. Answering his call, she scooted up to the flybridge.

"Hold this steady for me, will ya?"

Without questioning him, she slid her hand next to his on the steering wheel and watched him descend to the front of the boat. She could just make out his silhouette in the cloud-covered moonlight, but the sound of him dropping the anchor was distinct. Five minutes later he was back by her side, testing the security of the hooks buried deep in the sand. Apparently satisfied with his first attempt, he turned off the motors, flipped multiple switches, and turned to her. "I'll meet you downstairs."

Willa worked her way down the starboard side, stopping in front of the slider to the salon. They had both been careful to keep the interior closed while the boat was running, and they could blast the air conditioning with impunity. She stood for a moment, waiting for him, the thoughts in her head taking more laps than the cars at the Daytona 500. Fingers crossed that he was in a good mood.

"You could have gone in."

"Yeah, I know. Didn't want to waste any of the cool air."

Damian looked around the rear deck. "Everything of value locked up out here?"

Willa nodded in silence.

"I say we lock ourselves in for the night. I'm too tired for food, but I sure would like a couple shots of rum. How 'bout you?"

"A little bit of wine sounds like the perfect sleeping tonic to me." Willa smiled at him as she opened the door, welcoming the cold slap of air.

With no traces of the coins to spur a riot, Willa let herself relax as she reached into the cupboard. Damian slid behind the table, settling into the generous padding of the banquette seats, smiling when she passed him an open bottle of Pusser's Gunpowder and a double shot glass. But instead of pouring herself a glass of wine, Willa filled a pint glass with sparkling ice cubes, a sizeable serving of pineapple juice, a big splash of orange juice, and another of cream of coconut. Once all of those ingredients wove their way through the cubes, she enjoyed the colors created and the way the different weights of fluid painted the inside of her glass. Sliding onto the banquette to sit kitty corner to Damian, she hoisted his bottle of Gunpowder Rum and added a generous portion of the alcohol.

"Aye, lassie. Going for the Painkiller, I see."

She laughed at his weak pirate voice.

"You forgot the nutmeg." His pirate imitation had completely disappeared.

"The hell with it. I just want to drink."

Damian raised his newly empty shot glass to hers. "I second that."

They both sat quietly in the dim light of the salon, each enjoying their beverage. After a few minutes, Damian finally spoke up.

"Did I ever tell you about the night we all went camping?"

"Willa looked at his eyes. "What are you talking about?"

"In college. All the house mates decided it was a warm September night. Besides, we were bored. The trouble was, we didn't have any tents, just sleeping bags."

Willa shook her head slowly, trying to figure out which direction Damian's tall tale was headed in.

"It was your basic drunken bonfire at the edge of the woods. We didn't even know whose property it was, but we didn't care. Anyway, everybody was fed up with all of Harley's stories about his big, happy family and all his other goody-two-shoes blah, blah, blah when he slides off the log we were sittin' on. One second, he's talking and the next he's on the ground with his head resting on the log."

Damian pulled the Gunpowder across the table and refilled his double. He pushed the bottle back to Willa while running his hand over his drawn-out face.

"It was pretty funny. We tried to wake him, but he was out cold. Then one of the guys suggests we strip him of his clothes and roll him into his bag, buck naked." Damian started laughing and took a swallow of hooch. "The next morning, we all get up, except Tim, who's still hugging the log and snoring up a storm."

Willa tried not to laugh thinking back to her earlier thoughts regarding CPAP machines, but Damian didn't notice.

"So, we're all loaded up in Garret's car—I think that was his name—including Tim's clothes and sneakers. We're backing out onto the road when another car comes flying around the corner, laying on the horn at us. Harley jumps right up, and his sleeping bag goes south, dropping right around his feet. The funny thing is, he doesn't know his turtled manhood is making its debut in Nowhere'sville USA. We laugh like hell, toot the horn, and wave goodbye to him."

Willa's eyebrows shot into her hairline.

"Don't worry, that other car was there, and it was filled with college girls still out raising hell from the night before. And they all watched him trip over his sleeping bag and face plant into the grass. He had to hitch a ride with them back to town, with that bag wrapped around his ass."

Damian let out a few more bellows and then threw back the double shot of rum. "Everyone on campus knew about it. And it took him months to live it down."

"Pretty much a freshman hazing, huh?"

"Yeah. And now that I've got that outta my system, I'm sure you have lots of questions Willa. The problem is, the more I tell you, the more danger you may be in."

"From Tim?"

"No, darlin'. The other side of the law."

"Start with this boat. How long have you owned it?"

"About three years. It was a custom order from a company in France. It's got a combination of specially shaped racing hulls and larger engines than the standard live-in catamaran."

"That's why you've been able to push it so hard?" She looked at his eyes, not sure which emotion she saw there.

"Yeah, the *No Bananas* and I have a pretty tight bond. I know what it can do."

"And you live on it, right?"

He gave her a single nod in answer.

"And that's why you always stayed at my place, but never invited me to yours?"

"Yup. You just never struck me as a dock girl. You've got way more class than a lot of the women I come across."

Willa drew in a deep breath before asking the one question that had been nagging her, maybe for months. "Are you the dealer, or the mule?"

Damian looked down at his hands, his loose, blonde hair covering much of his face. After a few seconds, his eyes met hers. "This is what I meant about the danger zone for you, Willa. I've been both, but mostly the mule. And I didn't want you to ever find out."

"Why?" After the way he had treated her over the past three days, she was having trouble believing that he was truly concerned for her welfare.

"Because I never wanted to see that look in your eyes. That disconnected one."

"You know we're done, right?"

"Oh hell, I thought we were done before you got on this boat. I was real surprised when you agreed to come with me. I mean, you've been pushing me away for weeks now. Ever since...."

"Don't say it, Damian. Don't you dare blame this on anyone but yourself."

"Can you deny that you've been spending more and more time with my college roommate?"

Willa paused for a moment before defending Tim. Now that she knew about Damian's nefarious business ventures during their trip, feigning ignorance to the chief of police would be difficult. Not only that, but now that she had seen his wound, she knew he ran with violent criminals. For the most part, they were people who didn't care who they shot. And frequently, their target was a cop. "Tim is a friend of mine. He joins me and Jenn for dinner sometimes."

"It's okay, Willa. Tim Harley is exactly the sort of man who should be in your life, not me." He reached across the table, engulfing the top of her artist's hands with his own. In his eyes, she found no animosity. Sadness maybe, but not ill will.

Willa wasn't comfortable telling Damian about her

attraction to Tim. Since Damian's sexual proclivities trended on the darker side, she wasn't interested in him making suggestions about any future love life she might share with Tim.

"I need to go to bed." She rose from the table, put her glass in the sink, and all of the Painkiller ingredients in the refrigerator. Damian pulled the bottle of rum closer to him when she reached for it.

"You take the primary cabin; I'll bunk up here. That way, I'll be right by the door in case someone boards during the night.

DAMIAN ALREADY HAD the cat under full power when Willa surfaced. To say that she'd slept well was an extreme understatement. And though she'd love to blame it on the rum, she'd only had one drink. In truth, formally breaking up with him was what she needed. She knew she'd internally detached from Damian weeks before—maybe even before Tim had arrived in Banyan Tree Bay. Most of the time she'd been around Damian, they'd shared a great deal of laughter, and some pretty hot sex. But it wasn't a true relationship. It was a booty call. And after the past three days, her desire for him had jumped overboard without a life jacket. At this point, her desire for Damian was fish food somewhere along the north shore of Puerto Rico.

Making her way to the flybridge balancing two cups of coffee, Willa paused on the small steps to enjoy the day. They were cruising through open water with only clear skies, brilliant sunshine, and what she thought of as sea diamonds as their company. Knowing she would sleep in her own bed tonight was probably adding to her good mood, but she was tired of analyzing and just wanted to be present.

"Hey, sleepyhead. Thanks." Damian grinned as she handed him the coffee.

"Such gorgeous weather."

"You bet. At the rate we're traveling, I hope we'll be crossing the Keys and Route 1 at the Channel 5 Bridge around dinner time. That's if we don't stop."

"Will we need fuel?"

"Nope, yesterday's second stop completely topped off the tanks."

"Then I say let's go for it. I can whip together cold food for meals if we need them."

With a companionable silence cocooning them, they drank their coffee and watched the water. If Damian needed a break, he'd flip it to autopilot, leaving her in charge. Willa had counted the hours by watching the position of the sun from her perch at the top of the catamaran.

On a fair-weather day, having water surround her was an exhilarating place to be. Her vivid imagination took a deep dive and the *No Bananas* morphed into a pirate ship named the *Assassin*. Willa laughed at the idea of being at the helm of the massive wooden ship full of men, gunpowder, and gold. She stood behind the steering wheel of the *No Bananas* with her loose hair flying on the wind, shouting commands to her crew with her best pirate voice.

"Aye, maties. Scrub that deck. Leave no sticky trace of the villains we annihilated this morning when they tried to board this fine vessel."

With the salt air kissing her face, tears of joy filled her eyes as Willa thought of her father and the rich childhood he had given her.

When she saw Damian waving to her from the front, Willa was delighted to see the pod of dolphins to the starboard side, happily leaping and squealing their approval. Intent on watching them, thinking about Tim and if he'd find delight in the antics of the dolphins, Willa didn't notice Damian until he sat on the bench beside her.

"Hey, Gilligan," he gave her bottom a playful swat.

"Don't you go talking about sunken ships now, matey. If I squint really hard, I can see land. There will be no capsizing on my watch." She laughed at the surprised look on his face.

"Nor on mine. While we may float in salt water, I'd rather not be shark food." Handing her a bottle of water, Damian encouraged her to sit on the bench while the cat was flying on auto.

"Where did you learn your nautical skills?"

"My dad."

"And why did I not know this?"

"Probably for the same reason I didn't know you

owned a boat. Let alone a beautiful catamaran that moves through the water like a wicked mofo."

For the remaining hours of their trip, Willa and Damian finally had the conversation they probably should have had within the first weeks of meeting. She wasn't sure she wanted to know if she could have fallen in love with him because the pieces she knew of him now were laced with too much illegitimacy. Willa was many things, but a criminal wasn't one of them.

Chapter Twenty-Three

"Does it ever cool off around here?"

Tim saw a side of his brother that was starting to rub his nerves raw. He couldn't remember the last time his twin had sounded so whiney—maybe when they were about six years old?

"Well, if we had a key, we could probably start this rig and have some air conditioning. But considering that we're actually trespassing, it's probably not a good idea. And yeah, the temps will drop to about eighty-five around two in the morning."

John grumbled softly but stayed hidden in the dark corner of the commercial catamaran's cockpit lounge. A few heartbeats later, Tim knew the instant his brother also heard the footsteps approaching from the seaward end of the dock.

Tim's eyes remained on the lone figure that entered the soft yellow glow thrown by the ancient sodium light. His stomach felt like a rock dropped into it when he realized that it was Willa. *Why is she out here by herself? That selfish bastard. Is he using her for a shield?* Tim didn't have the answer yet, but he knew his body coursed with rage over Willa walking unprotected along the aluminum, talking to herself. Once she was two light posts up the dock, John finally spoke.

"Is that your girl?" His soft question pulled Tim out of his reverie.

"She's not my girl," Tim spat back at him in a restrained whisper.

"Oh, methinks you do protesteth too much. You are so into her." His chuckle was a little louder now that she'd gone out of sight.

"Jackass. If you're going to quote some cockeyed version of Shakespeare to me, at least do it with an English accent." Using flippancy as a protective shield, Tim had to admit that his brother was right. Willa had a firm hold on him and his heart.

The vibrating of Tim's phone interrupted their brotherly bickering. Still in his corner under the hardtop, he pulled out the phone to check it, thankful that he'd set the brightness level to nearly zero.

We've only seen the woman. You?

Tim checked the time before answering Monica.

Us too. It's almost 2300. Check with the team to see if we have volunteers to spend the night on surveillance.

Already done. Wright, Ortiz, Infante, and Ballios are ready.

She was an excellent officer and manager. Two traits that, in his experience, rarely came together in one person. He crossed his fingers that she would stay put in the BTBPD, resisting the lure of a promotion elsewhere. When this case wrapped, he needed to approach the commissioner about an elevated position to keep her happy.

Thanks. Send the others home in fifteen-minute intervals just in case Buck is hidden among us.

10-4

"Dearborn has this under control, we can head out." He heard his brother holstering the Sig Sauer nine millimeter that Tim had loaned him from his personal collection, since he knew John held Florida and Utah permits. "You go first, and I will follow you in five."

Without saying a word, John hopped over the side of the boat, his feet barely making a sound on the metal dock as he made his way to shore. Watching the time, Tim followed him as planned, wondering which boats his crew peered at him from. He wanted to laugh because he was sure they couldn't tell the difference between him and his identical twin.

AS WILLA TURNED off Beachside Promenade, her eyes scanned the windows over the gallery, finding herself a little let down to see them all dark. She wasn't sure what she had hoped for, but she knew that hanging out with Tim was not a smart move right now. Not tonight when her emotions were so raw.

Once she and her car were secure, Willa turned the lights in the apartment as low as she could. Drawing the shades, she dropped her knapsack on the floor in her bedroom, stripped to her birthday suit, and stepped into the shower. When one is playing in the water, even on a boat, the slight stickiness of sea air is part of the ambiance. But after the experience she'd just had and the knowledge she carried, she needed desperately to scrub her skin, as if it would purge her mind.

The hammering heat of the shower made her skin raw, causing Willa to spin the faucet and stand in the steam, breathing deeply to draw in the cleansing aroma of the eucalyptus shower steamer dissolving at her feet. Once she'd dried off, she covered her body with her favorite moisturizer, Sweetgrass from Beekman 1802. Willa pulled a silk caftan over her head and softly padded to the kitchen.

Comforting her hands with a hot mug of chamomile

tea, she slid onto the couch, eyeballing her cell phone on the coffee table, which she hadn't looked at in hours. She had just hammered her way through a hailstorm of bullets, both literally and figuratively. What she needed was to quietly hunker down, alone. Turning on the television, she lost herself in some sort of championship cooking show, having no idea who the competitors were. When she'd nearly drained her cup, Willa finally picked up her phone. Her only intention was to send Jenn a text message and then shut it off until tomorrow.

> Hey, home safe. Sorry if I scared you. Thanks for taking care of the store. Tired. Going to bed.

Dropping the phone on the table, Willa shuffled to her bed, leaving on the comforting lighting throughout her home. Stepping out of her caftan, she slid between the crisp, clean sheets she had thought to put on before traveling. Returning to the comfort and familiarity of her own bed, regardless of where she'd been, was one of her favorite things in life. Sinking into the plush luxury of her pillow, Willa gave in to a much-needed secure sleep.

TUESDAY MORNING STARTED SLOWLY in Banyan Tree Bay. With most of the tourists gone and the local kids back in school, early September was pretty peaceful in southwest Florida. Except for hurricanes—those were always a concern.

Since the Harley brothers were early risers, they were both on their third cup of coffee when the commissioner knocked on the open door of Tim's office.

"Got any extra chairs?" The older man chuckled as Tim and John jumped to attention. "Easy gentlemen." Theo Rivers pointed to the table where both had been working. "Sit, sit. I'll take the black leather one behind the chief's desk."

"Theo, I thought our meeting was in your office at ten." Tim squinted at his supervisor.

"That's what my calendar says also. But since I was already up and dressed, I thought I'd get a start on my day. Even though the streets are quiet, my calendar is not. And now that Labor Day has passed, primary season is about to explode all over the state."

Tim had forgotten about politics. Albany was pretty much a one-party town and there was rarely any local competition. Even though the location was one where people lived and breathed the loggerheads of political agendas and money because of the state capitol, police work didn't play in that swimming pool. He wasn't naive; of course the very top brass were politicians, even in Banyan Tree Bay. But the victims and criminals were not, and police work couldn't be either.

"So, if you'll give me a brief update now, we might be able to skip that ten o'clock."

"Of course. The first thing you need to know is that our chief suspect did not return from the Caribbean last night as scheduled. The passenger he had at departure appears to have been dropped off, alone. We didn't approach her because she's not a target of our investigation at this point." Tim kept his next thought to himself.

And hopefully never will be.

John was correct—Tim cared about Willa. But until they resolved the case, he couldn't do anything about it.

Pushing his personal thoughts aside, Tim continued to update Theo. "Also, I received a phone call this morning from the chief of police in Key West. One of our prime suspects spent the holiday down there living large and shooting his mouth off. They're keeping him under surveillance until they hear back from me." Tim stood from the table, moving to the window facing the Gulf.

"This is the guy who owns the marina?"

"Yes, sir. It is." Tim glanced at the commissioner. "And John's got an update from New York."

Theo gave the other brother a single nod, accompanied by a rumble of laughter. "You do realize that it seems a little odd to be speaking to the same face, but on the other side of the room."

John walked to the chief's desk, extending his hand to Theo. "Good morning, commissioner. We'll try to stand apart, so you don't think your eyes are playing tricks on you."

"Thanks. What's the word from up north?"

"Pasternova, the guy pulling the strings on Michael

Lyons, Leon Graves, and Damian Buck has been funding a new venture in the islands. Seems he has a line on a salvage team working on a dive off the western end of St. Thomas. Allegedly they have found a Spanish ship that was heavy with gold coming up from the coast of Venezuela while it was still controlled by a Spanish royalist army."

Tim's mouth gaped at what his brother just said, wondering who had written up the history lesson for John. World history was not a subject they had shared an interest in as teenagers. John had kept his grades just high enough to escape the wrath of the nuns who taught in their Catholic school, while Tim had gobbled up the knowledge. Even then, he'd wanted to travel endlessly—a dream he'd buried in the cold ground along with his wife.

"So, other than what we found on the first guy, we don't have any evidence to tie all these ends together, do we?" The commissioner's gaze shifted between the two brothers.

"No, sir. We do not."

Theo stood from Tim's chair and walked around the desk. Shaking each of their hands, he lowered the boom on their case. "If the woman seems to have been returned unharmed, I say we move this one to the back burner. Maybe we need to let the air cool a bit, luring the players back to Banyan Tree Bay. Now that the framework has been built, we just need to catch one of them with the goods." Theo stood in the doorway a moment before turning back to the brothers. "John, it was a pleasure meeting you. We really appreciate your input and connections on this. Make sure your brother files your expense account today so we can get you paid for this trip."

"Sir, that won't be necessary. Spending the past few days with my baby brother was payment enough." John inclined his head toward Theo.

Tipping his index finger at them, Theo left with a final valediction, "Have a good day, gentlemen."

When the commissioner's footsteps faded away, Tim closed the door of his office with a click of the antique, brass hardware and stood staring at his brother.

"Well, buddy," John clapped Tim on the shoulder, "Sounds like he just told me to pack my bag."

Tim started laughing. "You mean like 'here's your hat, what's your hurry? But don't let the door hit you on the ass?'"

"Pretty much, but a more polite version. Afterall, it is primary season, and we wouldn't want any bad press." John's state of hilarity turned his cheeks crimson and filled the room with laughter.

"Christ, we need to drop it a few decibels before he hears us from the street." Tim sat in the chair behind his desk. "What day is your return ticket for?"

"Thursday."

"Wow, you had that much faith in our abilities to solve this case?"

John leaned into his knuckles where he had rested

them on top of his brother's desk. "No, Tim. I had that much faith in you knowing how to do your job. You're a good cop, and you have a few top-level investigators working for you. All I did was confirm a few things about Pasternova."

Tim resisted the urge to break eye contact with his brother, the person who had always been his number one cheerleader. "Thanks for saying that, John. With you by my side these past couple of days, I found where I had hidden my self-esteem."

"Now, my wife and kids don't expect me back for almost two whole days. And since she's got her mother there, I don't see a reason to race home. If you can get away from work, I think the Harley brothers need to go freckle-out in that water." He pointed to the glass like surface of the Gulf of Mexico.

"Noooo doubt." Tim scooped up both of his phones and held the door. Surprised by his assistant's early arrival, he turned his brother around. "Adrian, this is my brother, John. And before you ask, yes, we're identical."

Adrian bobbed his head, causing the thick curl of green hair to flex, and shook John's extended hand. "It's nice to meet you, sir."

"I'm a civilian now, so it's just John. It's nice to meet you as well."

Before turning away, Tim tapped the top of his own head and smiled. "I like the green the best."

Adrian smiled beatifically as the brothers left to defy the first rule their mother had set—don't get sunburned.

Chapter Twenty-Four

In the three weeks since Tim had watched Willa step out of the shadows on the dock at Islands & More, he hadn't seen her in person. Her answer to each text he had sent was the same:

So busy catching up on projects.

At night he sat quietly, hoping to hear her moving about in her apartment on the other side of the wall from his. But the woman truly knew how to move on cat's feet.

Jenn had confirmed that Willa was fine, that she was indeed busy because Jenn had taken three new commissions in her absence, and that she didn't know why he was getting the same response each time from Willa.

None of that made him feel better. As matter of fact, even asking Jenn made him feel like a seventeen-year-old boy with acne passing notes in class. And he wasn't. He was a mid-forties-professional who had never experienced bad skin.

Tim missed her laughter, her smile, and the sweet citrusy scent that seemed to travel with her. The time for evasion on Willa's part was over.

Trotting down the stairs that paralleled hers, his footsteps intentionally clomping loudly, he made sure that she heard him. With his hand poised to knock on her door, Tim heard the security camera overhead as it clicked and moved. He gave it a bold wink and rapped his knuckles on the dense wood. It took a few moments, during which time Tim questioned his decision to see her about six times, but the door finally swung open.

Overwhelming joy filled his heart when he saw Willa. As they stood staring at each other for a few speechless moments, his gaze traveled from head to toe, taking in the chestnut running through the black strands of her messy topknot, the loose tank she wore with a pair of running shorts, her long tan legs and bare feet, the aroma of fresh paint comingled with what he considered her signature scent. If someone asked Tim to describe how he felt in that nanosecond, he probably would have laughed and told them to read a romance novel.

"Hi." He held up a single hand.

Watching the lines develop around her mouth and eyes, he could tell she suppressed a smile. "Hi." But she made no move to invite him in.

"You got a minute?" Tim moved his right hand behind his back so she couldn't see that he'd crossed his fingers.

As if debating with herself, she blinked at him a few times and then pushed the door back. "Yeah, come on up."

Tim stepped inside the doorway, waiting for her to close and lock the first one. Watching her flip multiple locks into place, he didn't realize she was so careful about security that it bordered on neurotic. At least it would help protect her if Damian and his cohorts had reason to come calling.

Without another word, Willa jogged up the inside steps to her apartment. Tim resisted the urge to salivate at the sight of her well-muscled legs and bottom, her derriere playing peek-a-boo with him from behind the smooth fabric of the shorts. Raising his eyes to the ceiling, he wished to anyone listening that the visit would go well. In the deepest part of his heart and soul, he didn't just want a relationship with Willa, he needed one. In her absence, Tim had made peace with how barren his life had been without her. God willing, she would confess to the same feelings.

SWAYING to her music and the flow of her muse, Willa felt Tim's footsteps pounding down the stairs as he left his apartment. Yeah, it was a Saturday—and yes, he was entitled to time off, but she wished he had exited their attached living space much earlier. The way he had every single morning since she'd come home from her lousy weekend trip. Willa had been very careful to avoid both men since then. Damian for obvious reasons. And Tim because she was afraid he would ask her questions. But her time for evasion had apparently run its course.

Looking at his handsome face winking at her in the security camera, she had the distinct impression that he knew she was home.

"Time to dance to the music, Davidson." She placed her brushes in the small jar of turpentine mounted in the tray of the easel. Yes, she knew the trend was to soak them in Dawn dish soap, but these particular ones had only been cleaned in the organic solvent.

Willa squashed her impulse to jump into his arms, to plant a thousand kisses all over his neck and handsome face, to tell him she thought she was in love...with him. True to form for the businesswoman she had pushed herself to be, Willa gave him a wan smile, hoping he'd decide she was busy and leave. But then he asked to come in. And that's when her fake bravado disintegrated. And now he was in her home. Right where she had wanted him to be for the past two months. And she didn't know what to say.

"Had a lot of work, huh?"

Willa inclined her head to the open door of her painting studio. "Yeah." *Such an intellectual response.* She tried not to roll her eyes at her conscience. "How about you. The Bay safe?"

"Ha." Apparently, he remembered telling her he thought the locals should just say "the Bay" instead of Banyan Tree Bay. She told him it would never catch on. "You do realize there isn't much danger lurking about, don't you?"

"Just wait until the snowbirds get here. Those damn northerners are trash-tossing, rule-breaking hellions like you've never seen the likes of."

Suddenly, Tim pulled her from where she sat, his hand to the back of her head, his lips scorching across her lonesome ones. And it didn't take long for her arms to reach around his neck, pressing her body against his, answering his tongue, stroke for stroke. When she thought her lungs would explode from a lack of oxygen, he leaned back, his lips taking their warmth with them.

"Oh." A tiny kitten whisper escaped her lips before she could think.

Tim held her face in his large hands, running his thumb across the swollen surface of her lips. The tenderness of his touch made her legs weak, forcing her to lean against him or fall.

"Willa, don't be mad at me."

"For what?" She tilted her head, staring at his incredible eyes.

"For impulsiveness like that. But I, I couldn't wait

any longer. I have needed to kiss you since the day we had lunch here. I know, you're in a thing with my friend. So, I've just been living on the scraps of time our friendship allowed me to have." He dropped his hands from her and stepped to the side. "I was out of line. I'll show myself out."

Before Willa could sort out his hastily delivered speech, she heard him going down the stairs. "Tim!" she screeched his name, racing to follow him. When she reached the top landing, he stood at the bottom, looking up at her. "Come back up. Please."

The instant he stepped through the inside door, she locked it behind him and pointed to the couch. "Sit." When he landed next to the arm on the left-hand side, she poked him in the shoulder, instructing him to scoot over. As soon as he settled, Willa wasted no time straddling his long legs, wrapping her arms around his neck, and reigniting the fiery kiss that he had started in the kitchen. When she felt the heat rolling from her lips down to her womanhood, she knew she had to come up for air, or move a whole lot faster than either of them needed in their hearts.

Leaning back as far as she could bend her legs, Willa placed a finger across his mouth. "Shhh, my turn, okay?" She watched the clouds of desire swirl in his eyes before he finally nodded. "First of all, I'm not in a relationship with anyone but me. Whatever was between me and Damian was fading rapidly when you arrived. When we went away over Labor Day weekend, I thought we might get to know each other better—maybe get the spark back. But what I discovered is that I had lowered my standards with him. I never made him accountable, and I let him belittle me and my culture, mostly because what we had was nothing more to him than sex."

"But I thought—"

She covered his mouth before he could finish the sentence.

"I'll do my own thinking, sir." She gave him a soft smile to take the sting out of her words. "When we were out on that boat, there was no loving, no cute stories about growing up. Nothing like that. I spent most of my time wondering what you were up to. Keeping my fingers crossed that you wouldn't find another woman while I was gone. Then the night we left to come home, a few things happened that made me realize that life with Damian wasn't good enough for me."

Tim pulled her back to his chest, kissing her cheeks, her forehead, and her lips before wrapping her into a welcome, comforting hug. After a while, Willa slid from his lap, pulling him down beside her on the couch. There were no more words spoken as they cuddled themselves into a deep sleep.

TIM AWOKE with his arms around Willa, her soft black hair wrapped around both of them like silken ropes. Looking down at her long lashes, he wondered how long the phone in his back pocket had been vibrating.

"Stop looking at me and answer it."

"What? I thought you were asleep." His chest rumbled against her as he reached the free hand around to his back pocket. "Shit."

"Duty calls?" Willa pushed herself off his chest, unwinding her hair from his other arm and standing.

"It does." He looked down at his wrinkled shirt and wondered if he looked okay to go into the station without changing. This time when his phone rang, it nearly fell to the floor when the vibrating surprised him. He tapped the green phone icon and raised it to his ear.

"Sorry to bother you, chief, but we just had a major development in the Pasternova case. I think you need to meet me at the dock A-SAP." There was nothing jolly in Dearborn's voice so this couldn't be good.

"Hey, Willa. I gotta go. May I see you later?" He saw her look out the window at the late afternoon sun.

"Um, yeah." She pointed to the door across the room from them. "I'll be in my studio for a while. I've got lots of housekeeping to catch up on in there with the flurry of painting I've done."

Tim stepped up to meet her, gently kissing lips he now knew to be luscious and magical. "It might be late."

"Text me when you get downstairs." Willa hugged

his neck and slapped his ass, sending him out the door with a smile on his face.

"DEARBORN, why am I meeting you here?" Tim looked around at the various squad cars and then saw an ambulance entering the parking lot. No lights, no siren. There must be a dead body.

"A couple of fishermen found Damian Buck's boat adrift in the Gulf, about a mile off the far end of this dock. They did not board the *No Bananas*, but they mentioned seeing a man inside the salon sitting at the table, slumped down. So, they anchored near it until the Coast Guard responded to their call."

"And what did our team find on the boat?"

"Sir, Damian Buck is dead. Apparently killed by a single gunshot wound to the head."

"Gangland?"

"Yes. TOD is estimated at five this morning. The boat's been tossed but there's no way for us to know what's missing, if anything."

The closer they got to the dock, Tim could see the uniforms of his own officers, along with two very tan men standing to the side, hands deep in their pockets, whispering to each other.

"You've got their info, right?"

Dearborn nodded.

"Unless the Coast Guard needs them, I say cut them loose. The fewer civilians we have around here the better."

"Sir, the Coast Guard already left. We have jurisdiction because the boat was found within three nautical miles of Banyan Tree Bay. But I have their cards to coordinate with them if need be."

Tim shook his head as he and Monica started down the aluminum incline to where the fishermen stood with the uniformed officers. Extending his hand to each of them, he looked in their eyes checking for shock or anything that seemed shady. "Gentlemen, I'm Chief of Police Harley. I'm sorry your fishing time was cut short by this unfortunate event. Thank you for calling this in and waiting around. You're free to go."

The two men walked to the top of the dock and crossed over into another section to board their own craft. Tim heard the motor before he saw a pontoon boat backing from a slip.

"Monica, make sure CSU has been very thorough with that boat. And, if the wreckage handlers can't move it into custody today, please make sure you leave two teams of officers here guarding it—one set on a second boat guarding Buck's vessel, one on board the *No Bananas*. Tell them to wear those little booties and rubber gloves."

"Yes, sir. I will."

Tim didn't want to look at the crime scene that was

Damian's catamaran. He didn't need to see his friend's blood to feel guilty about the relief flooding through him regarding Willa's safety. If necessary, he would bring her into the station for questioning, but no one would know in advance. Saving her life might very well depend on keeping her identity classified.

Chapter Twenty-Five

Driving across town, Tim rehearsed several ways to break the news to Willa. After the afternoon they had shared, he didn't expect her to be especially emotional, but she might be hiding something in her heart that Tim wasn't aware of. As instructed, he sent her a text when he was standing at her door. Less than a minute later, she led him back into her apartment.

"You are much earlier than I expected. The sun hasn't even set." She moved around in her kitchen until he spoke.

"Willa, come sit." He pulled another chair closer to him. The only part of her body that he touched was her hands. "I have some bad news."

She slipped her hands into her lap, intertwining her fingers together. Finally, she looked into his eyes. "What?"

"Damian died earlier this morning." He watched her closely as she pulled her hands against each other, the knuckles turning white with strain. But no tears, only a shimmer of moisture across the surface.

"Was he murdered?"

"Yes. Why do you ask?"

"He was shot at in St. Thomas. But the guy was a lousy marksman and only grazed Damian's side. I cleaned it for him when we got back to the boat. He refused to go to the doctor."

Willa loosened her fingers as she spoke.

"Is that what you were referring to earlier when you said there were things about him you didn't want any part of?"

"That was part of it." She moved her mouth and cheeks, twisting the soft skin when she paused. "It turns out that he lived on the boat. A few years ago, he had it built with supersonic engines and hidden compartments. He was some kind of drug running mule who traveled back and forth between here and the BVI on a regular basis."

"The mules are usually confidential employees who the top guys come to rely on, so they don't get their own hands dirty. Why would someone want to kill him?"

"When we were at dinner, I think he stole a pouch of gold coins from the owner of the restaurant. Wait just a sec," Willa held her index finger out as she dashed into her studio and back. "I have pictures of them. He was furious when I found the coins, but I think he forgot I took these."

Tim flipped through the images on her cell phone

while she continued to talk. "I did some research on them when I got home. Turns out they are part of an underwater wreck of a Spanish ship and super valuable. I don't know how he found them, or why. He about bit my head off when he caught me taking pictures to paint them later."

"Willa, have you mentioned any of this to anyone but me?" His mind flashed to the texts Jenn had sent him.

"Just Jenn. I'd been texting her the whole time because the trip was so awful. And then all hell broke loose when we were at dinner, and I got scared. She was the only one who knew where I was, and I was afraid." Tim watched as she fought the slight tremble of her lower lip. "Am I in trouble?"

"Not that I know of."

When her shoulders started to shake, her vulnerability was a punch in the stomach for Tim. *Damn you, Damian. You had to expose her to your shitty underworld. I'd throttle your neck if you weren't already dead.*

"But you might have to go into the station for questioning."

Tim pulled Willa into his lap as the first tears started to stream down her cheeks. With his arms wrapped around her, what started out as his honest attempt at consoling her, quickly heated up. Her mouth found his, her tongue teasing and poking, laving, and stirring their bodies into a frenzy. With his erection pushing against the very bottom he'd been admiring earlier, guilt reared its ugly head.

"Willa, wait." He held her gently, just far enough away to look at each other. "Are you sure this is what you want? Aren't you upset?"

"Tim, you don't understand. I've been waiting for this news for several weeks. Not that I wanted any harm to come to Damian, but I knew he wasn't smart enough for the water he was swimming in." She ran her fingers over the curve of his upper lip. "I gave up on him a long time ago. And now, I am completely free."

Sliding off his lap, Willa took his hand and led him to her bedroom. "I'd like to make love with the only man in my heart."

Alarms rattled through his head about every rule in police work he was breaking. Even knowing that this single evening might be the end of his career, for Tim, it was a hill worth dying on.

AS WILLA LISTENED to the news she'd expected for weeks, she prayed that Damian had felt no pain. Just because their relationship had failed to take off, didn't mean she was heartless. And even though they had formally split up from the relationship that never was, knowing that he was gone had been the catalyst to unlocking her heart for Tim.

Crossing her living room with her hand pulling his,

she hoped he fully understood that this wasn't a one-off reaction to the news. This was her body showing him what her heart had been trying to deny for weeks—that she was falling in love with him.

Willa flipped the internal switch controlling her need to overanalyze *everything*, stopped at the edge of her bed, and turned to face him. Without a word, she lifted his shirt up as far as she was able, waiting for him to take it the rest of the way. At the sight of his exposed chest, she grinned and ran her hands over the swirls of dark hair. Each time the flat of her palm skimmed his nipples, he sucked in a deep breath. And when she used her tongue to circle them, applying the occasional nip with her teeth, he released a moan so deep that she felt it in her own heat.

This man is so sexy. Sliding her hands down his rib cage and around to the flat muscles of his abdomen, Willa chanced a look at his face. She found his cheeks flushed with circles of deep cherry and his eyes heavily lidded. Without moving her gaze, she slid her slender hand into his shorts, enjoying the weight of his erection in her fingers. When she saw his lips part as if he were going to speak, she gave her head a single shake, mouthing the word "no."

After Tim raised her shirt, dropping the light cotton to the floor at their feet, Willa leaned her breasts into his abundance of curly, black hair, teasing the tips of her nipples with each pass across the covering on his dense muscles. His hands wrapped her face when he tipped her head back, his lips scorching her needy ones, his dancing tongue turning her core into a dripping treasure. When he slid her silken shorts over her hips and cupped her bottom, Willa wasn't sure how much more of his teasing she could handle before losing control. She pressed her mound against his engorged penis to show him she wanted—no! needed—him inside her.

He massaged the round muscles, occasionally slipping a finger closer to her throbbing womanhood. His tongue danced on her lips and then plunged deeply as he stroked across her wet folds, pushing the tips of his fingers a little deeper into her heat.

She heard herself whimper when Tim moved his hands so they hugged each side of her pelvis. Lifting her slightly, he slid her up and down, each time caressing her swollen clit with the top of his shorts. Each stroke was a giant fan across her sensitive nub, with his thick erection tapping the sensitive skin of her cheeks.

"Hold on to my neck." His softly mumbled words barely made sense to her when he momentarily slipped one of his hands away.

After what seemed like a lifetime but really was only seconds, Tim's tongue returned to her ear, lighting a new flame deep in her mound. "Oooh, baby."

For a millisecond, Willa's mind registered slight pain where his hands squeezed the flesh on her hips when he lifted her a little higher and leaned back. But then Tim slid her down, filling her begging deep recesses to the hilt of his massive rod. Within three strokes of his helmet reentering her, Willa lost her battle against the sensations flooding her body, with the half pain, half ecstasy scream of her release filling the bedroom.

When her body came back to Earth, Tim cradled her in his arms with a tenderness belying his size. Willa was vaguely aware of him pulling back the covers with one hand, placing her on the crisp cotton, and then straddling her on the mattress, his full erection leaning heavily between them, and his tongue working more magic on her breasts.

As the smoldering need in her re-sparked into a full flame, she lifted his chin, his pupils showing her his intense desire. Without a word, she pointed to the bedside table. Seconds later Tim was sheathing his solid manhood with a condom, and then kissing her some more as he shifted his legs so she was able to wrap her long ones around him.

With the storm cloud of her second release threatening to roll over them, Willa finally broke her silence. “Make love with me, Tim.”

For the remainder of the afternoon and evening, the sexy Irishman did just that—over and over, filling her body with his, and taking her heart along for the ride.

SITTING AT WILLA'S TABLE, it dawned on Tim that he could never walk away from her, even if he lost his job. During the hours of making love with her the night before, he had memorized every curve, every scar, and every special spot of her flesh.

Willa rode him like a young bronc buster, rubbing her clit along his penis with her back arched to cant her hips forward, and her nipples dipping into his open mouth. She taught him that she liked to take control at the beginning. Four or five times she would lift her hips just enough for the bulging end of his dick to miss the heat of her and then ruthlessly gorge herself on his manhood, taking him so deep inside of her that he could feel her moans vibrating over his length. And for as much as Tim wanted to set his own speed, he loved watching her face as her orgasm worked its way through, her clenching muscles massaging him into his own intense and uncontrollable release.

"Wil."

She looked over the rim of her third steaming cup of coffee.

"I need to meet with the commissioner today, give him an update on the case."

"But it's Sunday." She leaned back in her chair, holding the mug between them.

Tim felt like it was a defensive move.

"It is, but this is a huge case. Honestly, this has way more people involved than Damian. And until the units we've been coordinating with wrap up their work, there can be no leaks. Commissioner Rivers needs to know all the details to update the mayor before the press catches wind of it."

Tim reached down for his sandals when Willa touched his arm. "Come on, I'll save you the walk of shame."

After she led him to the bedroom, she confused Tim by opening the door to the biggest walk-in closet he'd ever seen, stopping at a door in the back wall. Lifting a blue velvet bag of what he assumed was a floral sachet from the rod, his jaw dropped when she pulled out a key. Within seconds she had unlocked the first door and slid the same key into the second one. Before Tim knew it, he stood amongst his own clothing. With his eyebrows arched nearly into his hairline, he turned to Willa.

"These doors existed when I bought the building. I had them rekeyed and have kept them locked ever since. I'll lock it behind you."

Tim leaned down to kiss her, surprised once again by the talented woman. "I'll see you in a few hours."

"I'll be waiting."

Stripping off his clothes on the way to the shower, Tim heard the deadbolt on both locks slide into place behind him.

RETURNING from his meeting with Theo, Tim felt like he was walking on air. Not only had he relayed the conversation with Willa, but he also came clean about his relationship with her. Expecting to be told to pack his office, instead the commissioner complimented him on the case but threw in a smidgen of censor at the end.

"Tim, I have known Willa Davidson for years. She's a very talented artist that has brought a fine arts sophistication to Banyan Tree Bay, even if she can be an opinionated pistol. Treat her well, sir, or many of us will be happy to drop you where you stand."

As Tim left the gilded office on the second floor of city hall, the older man's words followed him, "buckle up young man, you're in for one hell of a ride."

The man's deep laughter echoed through the empty halls as Tim mumbled to himself, "You don't know the truth to those words."

When he reached her door, Willa opened it almost immediately, shoving him up the stairs in front of her. As they reached the landing, she pointed to her right. "Bedroom."

With the single word of promise filling his ears, he was blown away when she practically shoved him into the well-lit closet. Noting that both doors were open and that his clothes were hanging next to hers, he turned around, placing his hands on her shoulders as she opened her mouth.

"I don't want any doors, or locks, between us. I want us to get to know everything about each other—to laugh, to live together, to fight together, and to love together. Timothy Harley, I have learned in the last few months that not only does the ocean reveal its hidden treasures of precious metals, beautiful life forms, and pristine waters. But it also showed me just how much I love you."

Tim watched the gold flecks as they mingled with the greenish, deep brown of her eyes, knowing he'd met the one woman he was ready to build his new life with.

"I love you too, Willa Davidson." Lifting her up to wrap her legs around his hips and her arms around his neck, Tim knew she protected his heart with her own.

The End

Read on for a sneak peek at *Beyond the Rubble*, book 2 in The Secrets of Banyan Tree Bay.

Beneath the Rubble

THE SECRETS OF BANYAN TREE BAY: BOOK 2

When the glint from a streetlamp bounced off the metal covered knuckles, Turk was sure he felt the pain before they smashed into his face, driving his head into the exterior of the building. He might even have felt the second wallop to his jaw as his limp form slithered down the old brick surface, abrading the exposed skin of his back before he crumpled into a human pile. Lucky for Turk his masked assailant decided not to kill him outright. Instead, the guy left him to freeze to death on a pile of urine-saturated snow in the hellish streets of Detroit.

"FOR CHRIST'S SAKE, Lennon. Will you look at yourself? And you smell like a damn old toilet."

Turk tried to ignore the deep voice disturbing him. "Lemme go." *Why isn't this guy listening to me?* "Just let me sleep."

"Turk!"

Holy shit, this time the other guy's voice felt like a sledgehammer to his head.

"Wake up, buddy!" Strong hands pulled at his arms, forcing Turk to stand. "Oh, Jesus. You're in rough shape. I gotta call this in."

Even though the man's arm was around him, the voice sounded like it was in a can somewhere far away. "Officer down, Lexington and Grove. Ambulance needed"

For a minute, Turk wondered who the officer was that needed the ambulance. Then he realized it was him. Slumping against the large-barreled body that supported him, Turk decided it was best if he went back to sleep.

"I CAN HEAR you talking about me." A heavy white curtain yanked open, revealing his partner, Mike Riley.

"Holy crap, we thought you died." Riley leaned forward to give him a hug but was stopped by a single word.

"No." Turk watched Riley turn around to argue with the intruder, but the man stopped abruptly at a vision of loveliness in multi-colored scrubs. "Don't touch my patient."

"But he's my partner and I thought he was dying."

Turk wanted to smile at the pout he heard in Riley's voice, except his head hurt too much for that.

"Well, if you manhandle him, he might just do that.

For now, he's my responsibility and I want you to leave for a few minutes." She pointed to the open doorway. "Go get yourself something from the cafeteria. They're open for breakfast now."

After Mike stomped into the hallway, his attendant turned toward him, practically blinding Turk with a megawatt smile and stunning green eyes. "Good morning, James. How are you feeling?"

"Turk."

"Turk what?" She tipped her head, causing a long, blonde braid to slide off her shoulder, the end of it tickling his arm as she lifted his wrist, causing a light floral bouquet to float past his nose.

"Call me Turk. James is my old man." His throat burned as the words came out.

"Okay." She placed her fingertips to his wrist and looked at her watch for a minute. Then gently returned his hand to the blanket.

"Why am I here?"

"Mister Lennon," she paused a second and smiled. "May I call you that?" Without waiting for his response she continued, "You were brought in during the night with three broken ribs, multiple lacerations to the skull—one of which required ten staples—and a concussion." After waving a penlight in his eyes, she continued to speak. "I am Lynn Forester, Nurse Practitioner."

"When can I leave?" Turk attempted to push himself up in the bed.

"Hold on, I'll help you adjust." Once she had him

upright with two new pillows behind his shoulders, Lynn took a step back from his bedside. "Given your stats, I think you'll be here a few more nights. The whack you took to the head knocked you out for many hours. Your blood pressure and heart rate are still protesting. I assume the attending will want you to be monitored for a bit."

A single knock on the door caused both of them to look up at Mike Riley standing there with a paper cup in his hand and wearing a smile. "Can he have coffee Nurse Ratched? He's a much nicer guy when he's loaded with caffeine."

"You're hilarious. The answer is no." Lynn turned to Turk. "I will be back once an hour for the remainder of the day. If you need anything, tap the red button." She moved a large beige, hardwired controller to the surface of the table that covered half of his bed, then smiled at Turk. As she walked past Riley, Turk thought he heard a deep growl directed at his partner.

Riley stood at the door for a few minutes. Turk assumed his partner was admiring her retreating figure. No doubt, she was a looker. Not as young as many nurses he'd seen lately, but Turk didn't care. Admiring women under forty was a whole lot like leering at his own nieces or the kids of his friends. It just felt wrong on so many levels.

"When can I get back to work?"

Mike burst into a loud laugh, barely balancing the

paper cup he still held. “Buddy, you need a few days off. After your last injury, I’m sure the captain is already processing paperwork for you to be out for at least a month.”

Turk raised his left hand, pointing his middle finger at Riley for mentioning past history. Okay, yeah, he’d done one hell of a number on his right knee, requiring three surgeries and weeks of physical therapy before he could return to work. They wouldn’t even let him return to light duty because the captain didn’t trust him not to run out to join anything high octane that Riley was handling.

“What happened last night?” He’d lowered his hand after his partner stopped laughing at him.

“Long story short, we were in the Brass Eagle on Lexington around midnight watching a few perps when the big cheese, Wild Man Renaudo came in. When one of the perps got spooked and jetted, you went after him while I took care of the one trembling in the corner. Unfortunately for you, your guy was an ox on steroids, and he pounded the living shit outta ya.”

Turk didn’t need Riley to tell him how much of a beating his body had taken. Everything on him hurt—even his teeth.

“Why did Renaudo scare them?” Turk groaned softly at the pain that shot across his forehead when he furrowed his brow. But even with the head injury, Turk knew the case they were working on had little to do with

Renaudo, a well-established loan shark in the Belmont section of Detroit's northwest side.

"We're not sure. The captain put another set of guys on their tails after we released the one I had. He figures that they're skimming of the top of Wild Man's operation and owe him some money."

"So why am I still laying here?" Turk was busy pulling the blankets off his legs when Riley reached out, smacking his hand.

"Knock it off. I saw the gaping hole in your head. You're not going anywhere for a few days." Riley squinted at him, his arms crossed, pushing his broad shoulders back. "And you owe me a new Wolverine's sweatshirt. I can't get your Yankee blood outta it."

FOR TURK, the next three days were hell. How was anyone supposed to lay still for that much time? *Don't these people know about atrophying muscles and blood clots?* Of course they did, evidenced by the circulatory wraps on his calves that woke him up every hour the first night, and the young, chatty thing that made sure she flexed his legs on the hours the machine missed. Rest up? This was a freaking hospital, and by his experience, you didn't go there for rest.

"Lennon, how are you feeling?" Turk looked up at the man entering his private room, Captain George Duval.

"Hey, Cap." Turk gave a single nod to his supervisor. A man who had pulled his bacon out of the proverbial fire a few times when Turk had let his temper get the best of him. “Great. I’m ready to get back to work.”

“And that’s one of the reasons why I stopped by.” Duval looked around the room at the various beeping machines, many of which were attached to him in some fashion.

“So gimme all the reasons.”

“I wanted to check on you myself. Riley’s starting to look like a kid whose puppy ran away.” Duval laughed at his own quip. “Of course, he also mentioned coming to see you again for a few hours later today so he could get a glimpse of the pushy nurse practitioner.”

No sooner had the words left his lips when Lynn Forrester walked into the room. “Good morning, Mister Lennon.” Her megawatt smile was about the only sunshine Turk had seen in several days.

“Excuse me sir, but we need some privacy.” Lynn held her hand on the door, dismissing Duval from the conversation. “I will let you know when we’re finished.”

Turk tried not to chuckle as the captain sunk his hands into the side pockets of his dark grey trench coat. The man turned so quickly that his outer gear took on a skirt-like persona, the long panels swinging around his legs.

Unlike Riley and the other investigators who had come to see him, Captain Duval seemed immune to Lynn’s beauty. *Ha! Married men. Slip that ring over their finger and their eyes lose the ability to see another woman.*

Lynn and Turk chatted lightly as she went through

all the steps of checking his vitals. On the second day, he asked her why a regular RN or even an LPN couldn't be doing the hourly check-ups, saying it seemed like a waste of her talents and time. She had simply given an unladylike snort before saying, "Flattery will get you nowhere, sir." Much later in the day she said the Detroit PD had requested a higher level of care, mumbling something about a union contract. Since Turk's head still felt a bit spongey during the conversation, he let it go.

"Your numbers look good today. The neuro will probably cut back some of your meds later this afternoon."

"Does that mean I'm getting sprung soon to return to work?" He thought he saw a quick spark in her eyes, but it disappeared.

"Maybe your company can answer that. I'll send him back in."

Moments later, Turk was left with the pleasantly aromatic cloud that seemed to be her signature. He drew in a deep breath through his nose, holding onto the beauty with his eyes closed.

"You got another minute or are you napping?" Turk reluctantly opened his eyes in response to Captain Duval's question and pointed to the chair by the side of his bed.

"Now Turk, I know you're not going to like this, but don't get yourself all worked up."

His lips were set in a straight line as he tipped his head at Duval.

"You are being released tomorrow, but you're not

going back to the field. Matter of fact, you aren't returning to the station for a while." When Turk opened his lips to speak, Duval held up his hand. "Don't argue with me, it wasn't my call." He pulled a legal sized envelope from the inside pocket of his sports coat. "This is your paperwork to be on administrative leave for the next three months."

"Three months? Why don't you just fire me?" Turk's voice was so loud that Lynn peeked around the jam, holding her index finger to her lips. "What the actual fuck, Captain? You expect me to sit in my apartment for three months?"

"Look, Turk. I told you this wasn't my decision. But the brass think you need some time off to heal your noggin, and to soothe that temper of yours."

"Captain, this is my case. Me and Riley have been working it for months. You can't jack me away from it now. I'll be fine." Turk tapped his head for effect, causing a stabbing pain to the back of his eyes. Struggling not to close his lids until the marauding band of football players decided to leave his head, Turk continued to argue. "I can do light duty in the office for a few weeks. You know, handle the computer research Riley needs. Captain, don't take me off of this."

Duval stood. "I need to get to the station." He extended his right hand to Turk. "Enjoy some time off. You don't have to stay here and stare at the cold, grey environs of Detroit. Go somewhere warm. Come back when the snow is gone."

Snuffing out any chance of further discussion, Duval took his leave, closing the heavy wooden door behind him. Turk wadded up the envelope without even looking at the paperwork and threw it at the door. “Cock-sucking coward.”

Acknowledgments

To my niece Julie and her husband Seth, thank you for sharing your beautiful family with me and for helping out with my Thai language questions.

To my BVI family (Guy, Jennie, Steve, Pat, Rich, Gary, Nick, Compton, and Lincoln) – the laughter, the hugs, and the water are always on my mind. It's time to sail again!

To Maura and Johanna – three years since I left the office, and you still help me out. Thank you for that. You are the sisters that I adopted upon retirement.

To my editor, Wendee Mullikin, your knowledge and tutoring always improve my writing skills.

About the Author

Gracie Guy has been blessed with an eclectic and rewarding life, filled with family, friends and a passel of animals. She's a wife, sister, aunt, farmer, retired athlete who loves her bionic hip and gardener, who proudly calls Upstate New York her home.

Visit her website: http://www.gracieguy.com

or

All Author: https://allauthor.com/author/gracieguyauthor/

or visit her other social media sites:

amazon.com/Gracie-Guy/e/B06XZXCWL7

bookbub.com/profile/gracie-guy

facebook.com/GracieGuy.Author

goodreads.com/goodreadscomgracie_guy

x.com/gracieguy_guy

Also by Gracie Guy

The New York Journey series

A Fragmented Journey

The Journey Creekside

An Officer's Journey

A Cowboy's Journey

The Journey Home: Paying It Forward

Passion novellas

Her Irish Passion

Her Carolina Passion

His Highland Passion

Dickens Holiday Romance

Racing Through the Snow: The Christmas Derby

A Very Merry Monday

Wrapping Up Christmas—coming December 2024

Made in United States
North Haven, CT
04 June 2025